SPECIAL MESSAGE TO READERS

THE FATAL FLAW

When a young woman wakes with no memory of her identity, she is told by Charles Buckler that he has rescued her from a vicious attack during her journey to Ridgeworth to become the intended bride of his distant cousin, Sir Ashton Buckler. An impostor has taken her place, however, and she must resume her rightful position. Who can Elinor believe? Is Charles all he seems? What happened to Sir Ashton's first wife — and why does someone at Ridgeworth resent her presence?

ANNE HEWLAND

♦

THE FATAL FLAW

Complete and Unabridged

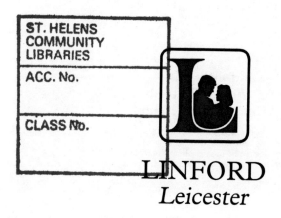

LINFORD
Leicester

First published in Great Britain in 2014

First Linford Edition
published 2015

A catalogue record for this book is available
from the British Library.

ISBN 978–1–4448–2549–7

Published by
F. A. Thorpe (Publishing)
Anstey, Leicestershire

Set by Words & Graphics Ltd.
Anstey, Leicestershire
Printed and bound in Great Britain by
T. J. International Ltd., Padstow, Cornwall

This book is printed on acid-free paper

Prologue

For Ashton, that terrible day could never be forgotten: dazed and shocked as he had clutched his wife's body in his arms; gently laying her down on the bed; hearing voices in the hall below; his landlady's curious face as she announced his grandfather.

Sir Bartholomew strode in. 'So this is where you hide yourself. I received your message. Married! It seems I am supposed to congratulate you. Is that what you hope? Hah! Never while I live. What possessed you? And to this girl, in particular.'

Ashton said, 'I sent no message.'

'You are not some grovelling clerk to marry where you will. You belong to a proud family. This marriage will not stand. I shall see to that.'

Ashton said wearily, 'There is no need. My wife is dead.'

1

Sir Bartholomew gave a great shout of laughter. 'And so you are well served!'

Ashton was overcome with rage. He stood close up to the old man, his face not an inch from his. 'I would do it again.'

'Would you now? And again without my permission?' The old man made a dismissive gesture. 'Enough of this. How did she die?'

'I do not know.' Ashton's anger dissolved as a great weakness swam through his limbs. 'I woke this morning and Sophia was . . . dead. Beside me.'

Sir Bartholomew narrowed his eyes. 'Unmarked?'

'What? Yes, of course.'

'Did you kill her?'

'Did I — ? No.' He paused. 'I would not.'

'You are certain of that, are you?' His grandfather stared at him as if considering what he was about to reveal. 'Because it would not be the first time for this to happen in our family. My own mother and one of my great-aunts, both died in the way you describe. It is the family curse. You have obviously had the misfortune to inherit it.'

'I do not understand you.' Ashton looked down at his hands. 'Surely, I would not. If I had . . . killed her, I would know.'

'Done while you slept, not knowing what you were doing. Your great grandfather and his uncle, both unconscious of the deed in the same way. This is why you should have consulted me before you married so rashly. I would have warned you. But enough of that. We must deal with the body. Avoid any hint of scandal. You are fortunate I was near at hand. I will see to everything.' His voice hardened. 'And her brother will need to be told.'

'I wanted to heal the bitterness between the two families.'

His grandfather snorted. 'And a good attempt you have made of that, I must say. What stupidity. But you need not concern yourself further with any of it. It will be as if this ill-starred union had never been.'

1

She was dimly aware of a steel-soft, angry voice. 'I will not be a party to this murder.' She wondered who was to be murdered — and why. And knew nothing else.

Until, surrounded by darkness, she was aware of the pain in her head as she was lifted and carried. At last she opened her eyes. In the bed where she lay, there was cool, crisp linen. Sunlight came through a small square window. And now a woman's voice, warm with kindness. 'You are awake at last. I shall go and tell the master.'

She said, 'No — wait, please. Where . . . are we?'

'He will tell you.'

Who? What master? Was this where she lived? Everything was strange to her. But it was more than that. Strangest of all was the numbness

5

inside her head, a lack of awareness of anything other than her surroundings. Apart from an unsettling feeling of fear, she could remember nothing.

The woman was back, bringing a man with fair hair and broad shoulders. She could see nothing else against the sunlight; he had chosen to sit with his back to the window.

He spoke softly and carefully: 'Welcome to my poor home. I am sorry you had to arrive in such difficult circumstances. An unfortunate introduction.'

'Difficult, yes. I suppose so.' She hesitated. 'Have I never been here before?'

'No. Your journey was cruelly interrupted, if you recall.'

'Journey? Was I making a journey? I am afraid I do not remember. But somebody spoke of murder.'

The servant gasped, hand to mouth. 'How terrible.'

'Terrible indeed,' the man said gravely. 'Such wickedness. Travel is such a dangerous affair these days.'

'It must be,' she said doubtfully.

'It was most fortunate that I was on hand. I heard your scream. The villains seeking to rob you ran off as I approached. I thought you dead at first. But I carried you here and with Mrs Haddon's good care, you are much recovered.'

There was too much to take in all at once. She tried to smile. 'Thank you. It seems I owe you my life.'

He leaned forwards. 'Do you recall anything of the attack?' He was looking intently into her eyes. She saw that his eyes were of a cool, pale blue.

She shook her head. 'No. Nothing. I am sorry.'

'Are you certain? We would wish to apprehend the villains if possible.'

She said, 'I recall nothing at all.' She stared back at him, with a rising sense of horror as she began to accept the truth. 'I believe I do not even know who I am.'

Sir Ashton Buckler frowned out of the drawing room window as his carriage pulled up outside. She was here. He must appear welcoming, of course, but calm; he did not wish to give any sign of the unexpected turmoil within. And unwarranted, he told himself. There was no need for this weakness. His course was clear. The promise his grandfather had demanded only hours before his unfortunate death had taken Ashton by surprise — but it was done, he had agreed to it. And now he would carry it through.

He smiled grimly, recalling the pitiful picture the old man had presented, lying back on heaped pillows, a handkerchief to his mouth. 'You came promptly. I thought you might stay away.' The dark eyes, however, were as malicious as always.

'I received the message that you were dying,' Ashton said evenly.

'And so I am. As you see. But there

are matters to be discussed.'

Ashton looked around the high room. 'Allow me to congratulate you. After all those years, Ridgeworth is in the rightful hands at last.' It was what his late parents had always longed for. The one thing of note his grandfather had achieved — and rightly so, for the estate had been badly run for years. Regrettably, there had been few signs of improvement since.

'You are pleased. I can see that. However, before you step over my bones into your inheritance, certain conditions must be fulfilled.'

Ashton merely raised his eyebrows, refusing to be provoked. 'That is your privilege.'

The old man smiled. 'I won this house in a game of cards, as you know, Mr Charles Buckler having no more wit than to accept my challenge. I can leave it where I will.' He coughed. 'In order to inherit, you must marry where I decree. To a Miss Elinor Buckler, presently living and working in Salisbury.'

'Working? Unusual. Is this lady a relative?'

'Distantly. No connection you know of. And she is employed as a seamstress.'

Ashton shrugged. He must marry and hope to provide an heir, presumably. After what had happened in the past, it made little difference to him who his bride might be. His grandfather was telling him a tale of how, being now on his death bed, he was repenting of some misdeed caused to the lady's late father. Ashton did not believe a word of it. Cutting into the old man's ramblings, he said curtly, 'I agree. But what of my unfortunate inheritance?'

'Unfortunate? Ridgeworth is assured. For you and your heirs.'

'Not the estate. And can there be heirs? I refer to the dark inheritance within me — and equally present in certain of our ancestors.' The old man stared at him, obviously perplexed.

'That is what you told me,' Ashton said patiently.

'Ah, that.' More coughing into the handkerchief. 'We will speak of that tomorrow.'

Hardly a surprise, after all the carefully engineered nonsense that Sir Bartholomew had made a full recovery only the following day. He insisted on taking a walk along the nearby river with his dogs, no matter that it was swollen and angry after an unusual summer storm. From the upper windows, Ashton had watched him set off and smiled wryly. He had thought, *Evil old man with his scaremongering, and all to get his own way. He will live forever.*

It was a shock when his grandfather did not return; when two of the men from the estate farms reported seeing him lose his footing, to be swept away. But there were few who would mourn him. Fortunately his grandfather's lawyers had been satisfied with the conclusive witness statements. Trust the old man not even to die in a straightforward manner. Certainly he had made no effort to regularise his financial affairs; Ashton had spent the first weeks after his grandfather's death putting those in order. Otherwise, who knew what a tangle his inheritance might consist of? He was still not entirely convinced of the legality of his position. Surprising that Charles had not made some counter-claim. If he did, the whole thing might tumble, although the old man's possession of Ridgeworth had been clear enough. *Be thankful for that, at least.*

All this had meant, however, that Ashton had been unable to search fully for this missing relative he must marry. He had begun as best he could before employing an agent to the task, and Granger had served him well. Miss Elinor had been found living in respectable poverty in the city of Salisbury, as his grandfather had suggested, and was informed of her good fortune.

And now she was here. He turned away from the window, not wishing to place her at a disadvantage. They would be face to face soon enough. He caught a glimpse of his expression in the mirror over the fireplace and grinned suddenly. This would not do. Glower like that and the poor girl would flee from him in fright.

His future wife was announced. 'Ah, Miss Buckler,' he said as the door closed behind Merrill, his servant. 'I trust your journey was not too tiring?' It was of no consequence, of course, as he was already committed; but he was relieved to see that the girl was presentable enough: mid-brown hair, a rounded face, a figure that might incline to plumpness now the restrictions of her poverty were removed — but no matter.

She smiled back, though no doubt the smile took as much effort as his own. This could not be easy for her either. Belatedly, he realised what she had just said. 'I beg your pardon? Your maid has absconded?'

The girl's grey eyes were troubled. 'I am afraid so, yes. When we stopped to change horses and have some refreshment.'

He could hardly prevent the scowl returning now. 'The maid I arranged for you?'

'I am very sorry, my lord. I am not accustomed to having a maid. I should have been more careful of her.'

He was aware of her tension and was at once annoyed with himself. 'Good heavens, it is not your fault. How could it be? My agent should have taken more care in his appointment of her. I will speak to him later about it — for of course you reported the matter to him.'

'To Mr Granger? Oh, no. He wasn't with us by then. At the last moment before we set off, he had an urgent message and had to leave us. He said to carry on and he would rejoin us later. A family matter, I believe.' She faltered to a halt, no doubt disconcerted by the surprise on his face.

'Is someone in the family ill? Not his sister, I hope.' It must be something serious to cause Granger to leave his duties in that way.

'I don't know. He didn't have time to say.'

'No matter. No doubt he will return shortly. Did the maid take anything of great value?'

'Great value? I do not have any such things.'

'Of course not.' He hoped uneasily that she was not about to cry. 'I mean, her motive must have been theft, surely?'

'Oh, yes. I am sure it was. There were just . . . some items of my mother's. Family items of no great value, but of great meaning to me.' She placed a hand upon her heart, an unconscious gesture that touched him. 'They were all I had left. There was a locket, in particular.'

He said, 'Nothing can replace your loss, I know — but be assured, you are returned to your family now. You will have jewellery, and to spare.' A clumsy attempt at comfort, he thought, when it was her loss of the sentimental items that mattered. She did not seem to mind, returning him a brilliant smile. 'You must still be feeling the effects of that ordeal. My housekeeper will show you to your room. We will discuss matters further when you are settled and feeling more refreshed.'

'Of course. Thank you. Sir Ashton, I am so grateful. My situation was very difficult; and since the sad loss of my mother, I did not know how I was to manage or where to turn.' She placed a finger delicately to her eye as if wiping away a tear.

'I understand,' he said curtly and regretted his tone at once. But women's tears unsettled him.

It was as if the tears had been banished. She nodded. 'Thank you.'

When the housekeeper entered, Miss Buckler also responded to the servant very suitably; he could not fault her manners or behaviour. He stared at the door as it closed behind her. He was relieved, yes. She was perfectly suitable. There was nothing that Aunt Pargeter could not gently mould for him as they had discussed; his mother's sister had been only too willing to help.

And the young lady was alert in responding to his change of mood too. Why else would she have controlled the approaching tears so rapidly? A little too alert, maybe. Did that response seem too calculating? No, now he was being unfairly critical. If this was to be the extent of his fault-finding, then he would be fortunate indeed, with little to complain of. They would deal very well together.

★   ★   ★

Now she knew the name of her rescuer: Mr Charles Buckler. She would cling to that. And the other details his house-keeper, Mrs Haddon, had told her: that he was an impoverished gentleman and a poet who lived alone in this picturesque house, little more than a cottage, seeking seclusion for his muse.

She ventured, 'He must be a very kind person, to provide me with this refuge.'

'Indeed so, miss.'

'Have you been long in his employ?'

'Long enough to know this is a good position and that, as you say, he is a kind employer.'

She thought drowsily that he could not be so impoverished, to employ such a respectable lady. Impolite to pursue that, though. She ventured, 'It was fortunate for me that he was there. And living nearby.' Mrs Haddon merely smiled and straightened the counterpane. 'This is so difficult for me. I still cannot remember anything. What happened when he brought me back? Did Mr Charles tell you how he found me?'

'Hush. You are to rest completely and not worry yourself with such thoughts. Those are my instructions. Mr Charles will speak to you and tell you all, I am sure. When he feels you are ready.'

She thought, *When my memory returns, as surely it must. When my head is healed and my limbs no longer ache.*

Resting here in this sun-filled room was pleasant enough, and with the attentive Mrs Haddon always on hand to meet her every need. Foolish to ask for anything more. Somehow she felt she was not accustomed to living like this and should enjoy it while she could. But when she tried to consider that idea and capture it, the thought slithered away.

Another day or so passed, and yet another. Surely by now someone must have missed her? Perhaps Mr Charles was making enquiries about her. Perhaps somewhere a family frantic with worry would be searching for her. Parents, or brothers and sisters.

She must do as she was bidden, and rest. Mrs Haddon had told her not to worry; but the more she tried to avoid worrying, the more she seemed to do so. The unquiet thoughts would not stay away. At times she could have wept with frustration.

After what might have been a week as far as she could tell, having slept so much, she awoke frowning. She had heard something. There it was again. A persistent knocking, somewhere above her head. The unsettling noise stirred her into action. She thought, *Enough of lying here like this, dependent on these kind people.*

When the housekeeper came in, she was sitting on the edge of the bed. 'Mrs Haddon, I do appreciate your kindness to me, but I can stay in bed no longer. I must get up.' She spoke firmly; she must not be deterred by Mrs Haddon's reaction. But Mrs Haddon was smiling.

'Indeed you must. And that is exactly what Mr Charles has suggested. As soon as you felt well enough.'

'And may I speak to him?' After that first brief conversation, which she remembered only hazily, she had seen little of him.

'Of course.' Mrs Haddon tilted her

head, frowning, as the knocking began again.

'Whatever can that be? It woke me — but I am pleased that it did. I cannot stay here forever.'

'Birds in the attic,' Mrs Haddon said briskly. 'Don't worry. I shall have Haddon see to it. And now, Mr Charles is waiting to see you.'

Perhaps he would be able to answer all her questions. This was good news and must surely bring hope. She had thought she must perhaps be seen by a doctor before this was allowed. But then, doctors were expensive — and perhaps one had been summoned when she was first brought here. Her face clouded. She should have thought of that. Never mind. Somehow she must reimburse Mr Charles. That he had asked to see her must surely mean he had discovered something.

It was as well that Mrs Haddon was helping her to dress, as her fingers felt like lumps of dough. She was hardly able to breathe, in a strange mixture of dread and excitement. What was she about to find out?

'Are you sure you're able to cope with this?' Mrs Haddon asked. 'If you don't feel strong enough, I can tell Mr Charles. I am sure he will not mind waiting another day or so.'

'Oh, no. Please do not. I dearly wish to speak with him.' She tried to stand up straight to prove her well-being; but all the same, she was glad of the arm the housekeeper offered. To her relief, the initial dizziness passed. She managed the stairs reasonably well and as Mrs Haddon helped her into the small parlour, she was able to smile her gratitude to her rescuer.

It was the first time she had been able to look at him clearly. Mr Charles was tall with fair hair and pleasing, regular features. Just as a rescuer should look, she thought. And his welcoming smile could surely only have one meaning. Mrs Haddon melted away, closing the door.

She said, her voice shaking a little, 'Do you have news for me? Have you discovered who I am?'

He bowed. 'Yes, I believe I have.'

2

She clasped her hands together to keep them from trembling. 'Please — tell me.'

'Let us sit down. Lest this prove too much for you.'

She allowed herself to be helped into a chair and waited while, all too slowly, he seated himself nearby and leaned forward, gazing into her eyes. In a low, firm voice, he said, 'You are Miss Elinor Buckler, lately residing in the City of Salisbury.'

'Oh.' She paused, waiting for some feeling of recognition. The name meant nothing. It might have belonged to a stranger. She could have wept with disappointment.

He was waiting too, still scanning her face. 'Do you remember now?'

'No. I am sorry.' She frowned. 'Are we somewhere near Salisbury, here?'

24

'Not at all.'

'Then where are we? And how did I come here?'

'It is an interesting story. You are a fortunate young lady, Miss Buckler.'

'I am?'

The story might be interesting but he did not seem to be in any hurry to tell it. 'Indeed so. A tale of family intrigue and skulduggery going back through the generations. But I do not wish to tire you.'

'You will not, believe me. Please, I need to know.'

'To simplify matters then: this concerns the death of Sir Bartholomew Buckler of Ridgeworth House, here in Berkshire. The old man charged his grandson, Ashton Buckler, with righting the wrongs done to another branch of the same family.'

She frowned, considering the information she had been given. 'But — he and I have the same name. As do you. You mean, he had wronged someone in my family? Or yours?'

'Exactly so. And I believe Sir Bartholomew's last instructions have bound Sir Ashton, as he now is, to seek out a certain daughter of that line and marry her. Thus making good the great financial losses that had been caused to his relatives.'

She said slowly, 'It hardly seems real. More like a novel.'

'It is all true, I assure you. And of course, you are the young lady in question.'

'I am? I cannot be. Surely not.' She shook her head slowly, considering what he had said. 'But if it is true, then I must consider myself as Elinor, and present myself to this Sir Ashton.' She was not sure how she felt about this new future which seemed to have been mapped out for her. She supposed she must indeed be, as the kind Mr Charles had said, a fortunate young lady. It was not easy to tell, when she had no idea of the nature of the life she had left behind. Or indeed, of what manner of man Sir Ashton might be. She had a sudden, unbidden thought that it was a pity Mr Charles was not the gentleman featuring in this plan. He was so kind, so gentle, so polite. And now she was being foolish. She blushed. He had his poetry and had chosen to live here in seclusion, or so Mrs Haddon had told her. He would not be seeking a wife.

Charles was regarding her kindly. He said, 'I know. It is too much to take in all at once.'

Elinor sighed. 'It seems so complicated. And I have enjoyed being here, quietly.' That was hardly true. She had too often felt restless and frustrated. Only now, on realising she must leave, could she appreciate what she would lose.

He was nodding as if he understood. 'I would have spared telling you this so soon. You still need to rest and recover.' He shook his head. 'But I am afraid there is more.'

She hardly heard him, occupied with her own thoughts. 'But if this Sir Ashton, my would-be benefactor, was expecting me, why has he not been searching for me? Why has he not found me?'

'That is it, exactly. That is what I must tell you. Sir Ashton does not know you are lost.'

Elinor frowned. 'But — what did he think when I did not arrive?'

'Someone did arrive. A young woman using your name and identity.'

'Oh!' Her first thought was almost of relief. Sir Ashton need never know of her existence. But no. Whatever was she thinking of? This Sir Ashton represented her one certain chance of security; she would be mad not to take it. She might not recall who she was, but deep within her being she knew the importance of financial stability. 'Who is she?'

'I believe Sir Ashton gave orders for a maid to be hired for you.' He paused. 'It seems that the girl has seized her opportunity and taken your place.'

'Oh.' She did not know what to say. 'Does she look very like me?'

'I do not know.' He hesitated for a moment. 'I have not seen her.'

She considered this, biting her lip a little. 'How have you discovered all this? I mean, if Sir Ashton has been taken in and does not know of it?'

'Ah, that is easily explained. The excellent Mrs Haddon has been instrumental in making enquiries in the neighbourhood — asking about new arrivals and so on. She has many contacts amongst the servants in the area, having been in service for most of her life. And her husband too. They are in my employ as a couple; I regard them most highly.'

'As do I,' Elinor said warmly. 'I shall always be most grateful to her.'

Charles said, 'It was Haddon who found you and alerted me. We brought you back here together. We are not far from Ridgeworth here, you see, on foot. Longer by road.'

'I had not realised. I must thank him too.' She straightened her shoulders. 'So, what must I do? Presenting myself

29

to Sir Ashton will be less than straightforward.' She frowned. What could she say to him? Would he believe her?

'I am afraid it might be difficult, yes. That is why I feel you must act sooner rather than later. The marriage is to take place, I believe, as soon as the banns are read. After the ceremony, it may well be too late. You could lose everything.'

If she had thought the original position complicated, this was far worse. Her thoughts were buzzing now with various possibilities, such as how Sir Ashton might or might not react. She put a hand to her face, only now realising the awful truth of what had happened to her.

'It was deliberate, was it not?' She remembered those sinister words she had heard: *I will not be a party to this murder.* 'They meant to dispose of me and continue with their wicked plan. How could they even think of that? I had done them no harm.'

He took her hand, shaking his head sadly. 'The world is full of villainy, I am afraid. Although how anyone could be so unfeeling as to make a victim of such a sweet-natured and beautiful young woman as yourself is beyond my understanding.' He drew her to her feet, saying in a low voice, 'I am glad beyond measure I chanced on the attack as I did.'

She nodded, her heart beating wildly. 'I too, of course. I will be forever grateful.' Before she knew what was to happen, his lips were on hers. She shuddered as she responded, relaxing against him, until suddenly he broke away.

'Elinor! Miss Buckler, I do not know what came over me. I cannot apologise enough.'

She shook her head, saying in a voice she hardly recognised, 'No apology is needed.'

'Ah, no. I do so regret this.' Charles put a hand to his brow, shaking his head. 'You must not. We must not feel like this. You are bound to Sir Ashton. Your future lies with him.'

Elinor said, 'But he does not know it. He knows nothing of me at all. There is no need for me to make my claim.'

His face was solemn. 'If I thought my unforgivable impulse had robbed you of your future, I would never forgive myself. Never.'

'It does not have to be my future, if I do not wish it.'

He groaned. 'I never intended to speak of this. My growing feelings for you overcame me. I had no right. None.'

'But if we both — '

'Hush.' He gently placed a finger to her lips. 'It is not possible. I cannot provide for a wife. I must make my own way in life — and have therefore resigned myself to solitude. I live here in my small house very simply.' He sighed in answer to her swift exclamation of sympathy. 'In the main, I do not regret it. And maybe you are regaining your rightful place on my behalf, so to speak, as well as your own.'

'I do not quite understand you.' Yet it was difficult to argue with the serious expression in the mesmerising pale blue eyes, staring into hers. She shivered, without knowing why. He had been kindness itself, and yet those eyes were ice-cold. No, this was foolish. The injury to her head had made her prone to strange fears. She had no reason to doubt him.

'Besides . . . ' He withdrew a little, his tone becoming more brisk. 'Would you have that base adventuress succeeding in her attempted crime? Not to mention her associates?'

Elinor shook her head. It was quite impossible to disagree with anything he suggested. It was as if he held the direction of her thoughts within his hands. 'No.'

'But for now, that is enough. You must regain further strength before we plan your arrival at your future, and rightful, home.'

Yes, she needed to rest. The storm of

emotion within her head and heart was almost too much to bear. She must now consider herself as Miss Elinor Buckler and convince this Sir Ashton of an identity of which she had no recollection. She sighed. A challenging situation indeed.

It was made even worse when on the following day and without warning, Mr Charles gave her some unwelcome news about her departure. He had been saying, 'Perhaps tomorrow, or the next day at the latest, you will feel strong enough to go. I do not feel you should delay any longer.'

She tried to control the quiver of fear below her ribs. Yes, she had been ill, but this continued weakness would not do. The attempt must be made. She had tried to sound calm and collected. 'Do you know Sir Ashton well? I gather his house is nearby. How long will the journey take us?' At least with Mr Charles to vouch for her, Sir Ashton would believe her rather than the impostor.

He gave a regretful smile. 'I am afraid I do know him. Which is why I cannot accompany you.'

Elinor stared at him. 'Cannot? But I had thought . . . I had not considered . . . ' She shook her head, closing her eyes. She must be strong. 'No, of course; I should never have assumed you would come with me.'

He was continuing calmly, as if declining an ordinary social engagement: 'I would very much like to, but I am afraid it is impossible. My presence would only work against you. Sir Ashton would be even less inclined to believe your story. It would be best if you did not even mention having met me. But do not worry; it is all arranged. Mrs Haddon and her husband will go with you. As Haddon was with me when we found you, this will verify your account. I trust him implicitly to mention only his own part in your rescue.'

She made a small, hopeless gesture with one hand. 'I am grateful beyond measure for all he has done. But my case is obviously weakened by my loss of memory. How can I convince Sir Ashton? What evidence can I present? Your belief in me is all I have.'

He smiled. 'Not quite all. There is something more. I have perhaps been remiss in not mentioning it. Mrs Haddon found something when repairing your dress, concealed in the fabric.'

'Concealed?' She paused, thinking. Was this something she should remember?

'Here. Two things, in fact. Take them.' He passed her a gold locket and a folded paper.

She stared, hoping to recognise them. Nothing came to her. 'Where did you say they were?' One tentative hand found its way to her throat.

He paused kindly. 'The paper was sewn into your dress. The locket was round your neck, as you might expect.' He said gently, 'I had hoped you might miss it and ask after it.'

Her mouth was dry. 'Is there a portrait inside?'

'See for yourself.'

She opened the locket, her fingers trembling. Inside were the miniature portraits of a man and a woman, their hair dressed in the fashion of twenty years ago. A wave of grief swept through her all too briefly before she was left feeling empty. 'I do not know who they are,' she said hopelessly. 'Are they my parents?' She did not know whether her grief was for the smiling couple or for herself, still adrift on a sea of non-recognition. If she could not recall her own parents, she must be lost indeed. She whispered, 'What happened to them? Are they dead?'

'I am afraid so. I did not intend to upset you, so I did not mention them earlier, when you were so unwell. Not until now, when there is no alternative. If it had not been for this adventuress and her false claim . . . ' He shrugged.

'You are right. If these are indeed my parents, I owe it to them to ensure that her wickedness does not succeed. And the letter? Where did you say I had it?'

'Mrs Haddon found it sewn into the hem of your skirts. As if you anticipated some treachery maybe.'

'Have you read it?'

'I am sorry. I felt I must, in my search for evidence of your identity.'

'Of course.' She hardly dared look at it. She unfolded the pages. 'Oh, it is a signed affidavit, giving evidence of my birth. From the Reverend . . . ' She peered at the crabbed signature.

'Greenwood, I believe.'

'Yes, I see it now.' Her heart was beating faster. Surely if she had seen this before, she would remember it? These facts must be known to her. She scanned the words: 'I ascertain that Miss Elinor Buckler, the bearer of this paper, is the daughter of Mr James Buckler and Elizabeth his wife, formerly Aysgarth. Elinor Buckler was baptised in the village of Laverstock, near Salisbury, on the 12th day of April, 1795. James Buckler being the son of Jeremiah Buckler, the brother of Bartholomew Buckler of Ridgeworth House in the county of Berkshire, or so I have been told in good faith.'

She could hardly begin to take it in. She read it all again, only to feel no wiser. This was who she was, all set out and signed firmly and strongly. She only wished she could remember being this person, or even feel that she was; the slightest tremor of recognition would suffice. And yet she must be. This Reverend Greenwood had said so.

'So you see,' Charles was saying, 'there can be no doubt. There is no argument against you.'

Elinor said, 'Yes. This must surely satisfy Sir Ashton. But how will the . . . impostor react when I arrive? If I have been attacked once, will she and her accomplices see me as even more of a threat now?' She was surprised to find herself discussing her possible safety in such a calm voice. She might be talking about someone else. Indeed, she felt as if this was all happening to another person altogether, and she was merely an onlooker.

'This is why you must go as soon as you can. The banns are not even read — and even so, they will be in your name and not hers. But this week she is accompanying an aunt of Sir Ashton's to London to purchase wedding clothes. So there will be no immediate danger from her. You only need to convince Ashton himself and your safety is assured. He will handle the situation from then on.' He laughed dryly. 'I cannot fault him for efficiency.'

She said, with a flash of insight, 'You do not like him.'

'Am I so transparent? I am afraid you are right. It is regrettable — but not strictly his fault. He and I are, shall we say, influenced by our circumstances.' He paused. 'I did not intend to tell you the whole of this; I did not wish to colour your opinions before you were able to form your own. You see, many men might consider I am as much a victim of the wrongful inheritance as you are. But unfortunately my family line was not included in the old man's deathbed remorse. He was only willing to repent in part, it would seem.'

Her hands tightened on the paper she still held. 'This is dreadful! How desperately unfair. How could Sir Ashton allow himself to benefit from his wealth and title, leaving you like this?' She shook her head. 'However can I marry such a man? I will not do it.'

'Ah, my dear, you are so lovely in your distress.' His face was once more close to hers. She closed her eyes. He said softly, 'No.' He moved away. 'I must be firm in my resolve. There is no gainsaying it. And some might say my position is due to my own foolishness.' He shook his head but seemed unwilling to explain further.

'But I must help you. I do wish to. What can I do?'

'The best way, if you truly wish it, is to accept your rightful place by Sir Ashton's side. Take it gladly. And when you are thus in a position of some power, perhaps we shall see. You may be able to ease matters for me with Sir Ashton, gradually, so I too may be restored to the family and accepted once more.'

'Oh, yes. I am sure I could do that and heal the rift between you.'

'Thank you.' He nodded gravely.

'But once I am at the house, until I have managed whatever it is I have to do . . . ' She stopped, uncertain of what she was trying to say. Only knowing she must bid goodbye to her rescuer and only friend. She did not know how she could bear it. 'It is a long time to wait,' she ventured. 'Will I not see you again?'

'We must not rush matters. That could ruin everything. You will have to trust me, my dear. I am sure something can be arranged to ease our parting. You have my promise.'

She nodded. Her task would be hard but yes, for his sake, she would do it.

3

Ashton bade his intended bride goodbye with mixed feelings; feelings which
she did not seem to share, for she took
his hand, looked earnestly into his eyes
and said, 'Thank you, my lord. I shall
make you proud of me.'

'Of course,' his aunt said, with every
appearance of enjoyment. 'I am
delighted to have such excellent
material to work with.'

He nodded and said all that was
proper; but as the carriage turned
through the gates, his feeling of relief
shocked him. Should he be experienc-
ing this lightening of the spirits at her
departure? Soon she would be with him
permanently. Of course, she had been
thrust upon him and he was a contrary
creature who valued his freedom, as his
aunt had always remarked. Only last
night Lady Pargeter had said, 'You will

settle to it, Ashton. Everyone does, one way or another.'

He had bowed and said, 'Quite so,' wishing to end the conversation. His aunt knew nothing of the past darkness he had suffered and inflicted, if his grandfather could be believed. He had been grateful at the time for his grandfather's efficiency, even though Ashton was now condemned to a lonely future. But should he have believed Sir Bartholomew so readily?

If so, what was he about to inflict on this young woman? But he had no choice. If he did not fulfil the conditions of the will he would lose Ridgeworth, and that must not happen. He would think of some way forward during the coming week. The will had stipulated only that a marriage should take place; nothing more. That might provide a solution.

He must not become too fond of his bride. He had been careful to remain polite at all times, but he suspected she had noticed his lack of warmth. There was something about her manner that was not quite right; for all her gaiety and enthusiasm, he could sense a wariness about her.

Well, the day before him was his own. And the next week at the very least, if not more. Arranging a trousseau was a serious business for ladies, he understood. He had resisted the temptation to tell his aunt there was no need to hurry back. There was every need. He must have the matter over and done with.

He shook his head. Who was he trying to deceive? If he had wanted haste he would have purchased a licence instead of suggesting the delay of the banns. No one seemed to have noticed. But it was a cowardly trick. Perhaps he would get a licence anyway.

He turned abstractedly at Merill's knock, still half-occupied in wondering how he would spend the day. 'Yes?'

'Two men from one of the farms, Sir Ashton. A body has been found in the river, it seems.'

'Ah! I will come and speak to them at once.' At last. It had been accepted that his grandfather had died in the river, but a body to bury would conclude the matter.

Merrill had left them at Granger's office. Ashton walked in briskly. 'Where did you find the body? Could you identify him?'

The two men took their cue from him and were businesslike rather than making any pretence of grief. No one had been sad to see the old man go. 'The water had done its work, Sir Ashton. You couldn't make out the features, but he had this ring. We took the liberty of bringing it to you.'

He nodded. The effects of a raging torrent, of course. To be expected. And yes, this was the distinctive signet ring his grandfather had always worn. There could be no mistake. 'Good. You did well. Where is he now? I will come and look, for the formality of the matter.' And then he could proceed with the funeral and burial. A weight taken from his shoulders; he was thoroughly glad of it. 'Wait for me in the yard.'

Merrill was approaching him yet again, however. 'There is a young lady asking for you, Sir Ashton. A Miss Buckler?' He managed to turn the announcement into a query. 'I have placed her in the library.'

'Oh?' Ashton frowned, unable to think who this could be.

'She has asked me to give this to you.' Ever mindful of formality, Merill had placed an object upon a tray: a gold locket. Ashton stared at it. No need to ask which locket this was. He could hear his new fiancée's words as clearly as if she were still standing in the room: 'Family items of no great value, meaning everything to me. A locket in particular.'

He took it from the tray, his mind racing. Surely he was not now to be faced with the thief herself, in person? A bold move on her part, if so. If this young woman, whoever she might be, had wanted an audience with him, she could have thought of no better way to guarantee his interest. 'Show her into the drawing room.'

He was standing before the hearth as his visitor came in, giving himself the best view of her entrance. His first thoughts were that she was slim and pale, with a look of determination. But in what direction was that determination to be aimed? He was appraising her now almost dispassionately, and making comparisons with another similar arrival only ten days before. There was none of the gaiety and self-confident charm his fiancée displayed, although this girl was dark-haired and pretty with an elfin subtlety that was more to his taste.

What was he doing? He was not conducting some kind of contest. And yet he must appraise her. If, as he strongly suspected, she was an adventuress, he would need all his wits about him to expose her. Surprisingly, he felt himself ready to welcome the challenge. He was more alert and alive than at any time since his grandfather's death. And particularly since he had set out on the journey of his imposed marriage.

He bowed his head as she bobbed. 'Miss Buckler.'

'Sir Ashton.' Her voice was soft — but he must not allow himself to be deceived by that.

He made his voice level, giving nothing away. 'I might have said, 'Yet another Miss Buckler.' No doubt you are to tell me that you are a relative of mine. I have a great many, it would seem.'

'I know nothing of that. Oh, you mean, I am not the first to come here?' She hesitated. 'Mrs Haddon told me as much. But yes, I do believe myself to be a relative of yours. My name is Elinor Buckler. You have the locket in your hand which was given to me by my parents.'

He glanced down at it. 'Yes, so I have. By your parents, you say? You are certain you obtained this by legal means?'

'No, I am not certain.' She raised blue eyes to his, staring back at him without blinking. 'Because I cannot remember who I am.'

He almost laughed. This was clever, he had to admit. 'Come now. That is too convenient.'

'Convenient? How can you say that? It is not convenient at all. I am adrift, lost. You can have no idea of how it feels, not to be able to remember who I am or how I came to be here, or anything before ten days ago. I am at the mercy of what people tell me. I am completely dependent on the kindness of my rescuers. Who in turn can only tell me how they found me — and the conclusions they have drawn.' She dropped her eyes, swaying a little.

A masterly performance. Most convincing. 'So tell me this tale you have been told. And pray sit down.'

She obeyed. 'If you wish, you can hear it directly from Mr and Mrs Haddon. They found me, have cared for me and brought me here. They are waiting outside.'

And expecting some reward no doubt. 'I shall hear their version of events. You may be certain of that. But first, I would hear yours.'

She glanced around the drawing room as if hardly seeing it, like a hunted rabbit. Was she to founder at this point? He shook his head. He should have been more cautious when beginning his search for the lady. He had enabled any adventurers to take advantage of the opportunity. It was unfortunate for this girl that she had arrived too late, with his search complete. He frowned. Or maybe fortunate, if she had known of the hidden darkness within his past.

She was beginning: 'They found me just off the main highway, in the woodland, where the downs begin. So they have told me. I have not been back. I had a blow to the head and severe bruising — as if I had been attacked and thrown from a carriage maybe.'

'Or thrown from a carriage and then attacked.'

She frowned, disconcerted at the interruption of her little speech. 'I beg your pardon?'

'Surely, we cannot assume anything. Not if you cannot recall it. Is that true? That you can remember nothing of this 'accident'?'

She met his gaze calmly. 'Yes.'

'When do your memories begin?'

'At something I heard. A voice — a man's voice, I think, although he spoke very quietly, saying that he would not be a party to murder. And then I recall nothing else clearly until I woke with Mrs Haddon sitting beside me.'

This much, he felt, was probably true. But he would not be so obliging as to admit himself convinced. 'Most dramatic, I am sure. The very stuff of a gothic novel. Pray continue. I am finding all this most entertaining.'

She glared at him but continued calmly enough. 'Mrs Haddon nursed me with all care and attention. I shall always be grateful to her. She and her husband made enquiries as to who might have been expected in the area and never arrived — and reached their conclusion as to my identity.'

'And so you have made haste to come here with your claim at the earliest opportunity.'

She closed her eyes. 'I wonder, might I have a glass of water?'

He must believe her, in her description of her injuries at least. She had seemed naturally pale on arrival but now her face was white and drained. He had been too harsh on her. 'Certainly,' he said gruffly, knowing himself to be at fault in this. 'I will ring for refreshment. I do not wish you to faint before me.'

She sat quietly until fruit cordial was brought and she was able to revive a little, to his relief. He said, 'Perhaps you have come here too soon, considering your state of health.'

'I had to, Sir Ashton, for news of your intended marriage is current now and I believe you would unwittingly be marrying the wrong lady.'

'Then it is most kind of you to so inform me. I am most grateful.'

She gave him an impatient look. 'You do not believe me. And why should you?'

'If you do not remember any of this yourself, how are your benefactors so certain of who you are? They have merely thought it likely; is that what you said?'

'Not merely, no. It was a matter of putting all the evidence together. I had no luggage with me; that was obviously taken. But I have two firm pieces of evidence to confirm my claim.'

'Ah, yes. The locket.' He knew his tone was not encouraging. He could still hear that phrase, *articles stolen*.

'And not only that, although you will see that it contains portraits of my parents. I also have this paper which had been sewn into the hem of my dress.'

'And discovered by the good Mrs

Haddon, no doubt.'

'Yes. So, please, do you recognise the portraits?'

'It would be most unlikely. I have never met the people in question. Indeed, had never heard anything of an Elinor Buckler, either, until my grandfather mentioned her.'

'But would you please look at them? There may be a general family resemblance.'

He did as she suggested, staring at the two people closely to satisfy her request, before snapping the locket shut and passing it back to her. 'I am afraid I do not recognise anything in them. But then, I do not see any family resemblance in yourself, either.'

'And in the lady who arrived before me?'

He smiled, nodding, pleased that she had thought to ask it. 'No.'

She sighed. 'Perhaps this will be more useful.' She took a folded paper from the reticule she carried and passed it to him. 'It is a signed . . . '

He raised a hand to prevent her saying more. 'I prefer to see for myself.' Yes, this was impressive. A clever notion on someone's part. And verifiable — which meant that maybe someone had not been quite clever enough. He refolded the paper and sat back. 'Very interesting.'

'So now you must believe me.'

He said slowly, 'Must I? How can I accept this when *you* do not know whether to believe it? You are merely accepting what you have been told.'

'How can I doubt it?' She hesitated. 'Mr and Mrs Haddon are good people.'

The hesitation had been slight but he had noticed it. He said, 'I am sure they are.' And just as certain that, whatever their story, they would have been well-instructed in it. 'And of course, I will be speaking to them myself.' He could often discern a villain, but there were degrees of villainy. It was by no means inevitable that he would see through them. Watching her face closely, he said abruptly, 'And I will then travel to Salisbury and speak to this Reverend Greenwood.'

He had expected her to be disconcerted but she clasped her hands together, eyes wide in what must be genuine delight. 'Oh, what an excellent idea. He will be able to speak for me himself. And of course, he must recognise me.'

'I was not considering taking you with me.'

'But you must. Please. All will be solved and in the easiest way. And I must surely recognise the town and my memories will return. It is the best idea possible.'

He regarded her thoughtfully. If this was part of her act, it was very accomplished. And there was something about her his present fiancée lacked. Against all logic and expectation, not to mention common sense, he found himself warming to her. 'Very well. You will stay here now, of course, and we will travel to verify your story in the morning.'

She frowned briefly. 'And the other Miss Buckler?'

'There are sufficient rooms here for any number of fiancées. It is fortunate, however, that the first Miss Elinor Buckler is currently absent, obtaining her wedding clothes in the company of my aunt.' He looked at her closely.

'I see.' She did not seem surprised.

'But presumably you knew that too. The worthy Haddons have been very busy on your behalf. You have timed your arrival and revelation to perfection.'

'Yes.' She sighed. 'I admit that. It is one of the reasons I came here straightaway, without waiting to become stronger, although that might have been wise. I wanted to be certain of speaking to you alone.'

'A wise decision, I am sure. And one that has succeeded in keeping matters simple. For the meeting between the two Miss Bucklers will provide an added interest to the whole situation.'

She said sadly, 'I know. It is not

something I am looking forward to.'

'And then I must make my choice. While a room is being prepared for you, I will speak to your companions. If you will excuse me.'

Once in the hall, he paused, frowning. With the first applicant, the possible danger awaiting his bride had hardly occurred to him. But somehow he was far less willing to subject this girl, alone and vulnerable, to the risk.

4

Quickly and efficiently, Sir Ashton's housekeeper was ready to show Elinor to the room which had been prepared. There was a truckle bed for Mrs Haddon, until a new maid might be appointed for her.

'Thank you,' she said as the housekeeper withdrew. 'Sir Ashton has thought of everything.' At least Mrs Haddon was a familiar face.

'Indeed he has. He obviously has a care to ensure you are correctly chaperoned.' Mrs Haddon's voice was approving. 'And he has already interviewed me to hear my view of your rescue. Not that I could tell him a great deal. I knew nothing before Mr Haddon brought you to me.'

Surely Mrs Haddon was being unduly cautious? 'Oh, I see. Yes.' Elinor found herself looking warily over her shoulder. It was not easy to keep secrets in a household of servants, she supposed.

Mrs Haddon was saying, 'And now Sir Ashton is to speak to Haddon, who will be able to tell him all he knows. But we have work to do, Miss Elinor. You will have time for a short rest and then you must prepare for dining with Sir Ashton.'

'Dining with him?' She had not thought of that. Maybe she had assumed that until her identity was proven to Sir Ashton's satisfaction, she would eat alone in her room. 'I have nothing to wear.'

Mrs Haddon smiled. 'That has all been provided for. See.' Arranged on a chaise longue in the dressing room were two dresses that shimmered in the light of the late afternoon. 'I am to apologise that they are not in the current fashion, and perhaps the silk is a little heavy — but we may contrive, I am sure. Which would you like to wear tonight?'

'I shall feel quite over-awed wearing

either.' Maybe that was the intention. And the whole insistence of her presence at dinner would become part of a test of her credibility. Maybe Sir Ashton had observed the usurper going through the same exercise. If so, she wondered how the other girl had conducted herself. And how she herself would.

After an hour of rest, she smiled as she regarded herself in the mirror. Surely she was too grand for an intimate dinner in this shimmering fall of cream silk? She would have thought it far more suitable for a ball. But who could not gain a measure of confidence, dressed like this? She straightened her back — and somewhere in her mind, a voice was saying, 'Always hold your head high. Never forget, whatever happens, that you could be a lady.' She almost exclaimed out loud. She had remembered something. But who had said it? Her mother, her grandmother? She closed her eyes, seeking the picture that might accompany the words. But it was like trying to grasp at a dandelion seed.

'Are you all right, miss?' Mrs Haddon put out a steadying hand.

'Yes. Thank you.' She gave Mrs Haddon a dazzling smile, half-tempted to confide what had just happened. But if she had imagined it, to tell of it might be a temptation to fate. But now she had a reason to hope.

She walked slowly down the stairs in the unfamiliar gown. Now she was not merely the girl who had been rescued, but someone else who walked in a dream. The brief memory combined strangely with the new attire, to build a new person.

Sir Ashton, waiting for her in the drawing room, nodded approvingly. 'Good. I see that Mrs Sewell and Mrs Haddon between them have found something to fit you.'

'I cannot begin to thank you. It is beautiful.'

He shrugged. 'Since there would appear to be two Miss Elinor Bucklers, it is only fair that I treat you both as similarly as possible. Dresses were provided for the other lady of course, and the attics and cupboards here are full of unwanted garments.'

'You are very generous. Thank you.'

'Generosity has no part in it. I am fulfilling an obligation and must ensure my future wife has everything she requires.' He smiled, softening the severity of the words. 'Whoever she may turn out to be.'

She smiled back politely. At times she did not know how to read him. But then, he must be feeling the same way about her, and with even more at stake, since he must prove her true identity and take the right wife. For better or worse. She sighed. No, this would not do. This was her path, this her life, whether for better or otherwise; and she must seek the best of whatever she might find.

He was continuing: 'And that being so, your choice of colour is fortunate, for these will go very well.' He was holding a small flat box in his hand and as she watched, slid out a necklace of green stones in a gold setting. And as she stood, mesmerised by the green flames that sparkled within the stones, 'Come. I will fasten it for you.'

'Thank you.'

His hands were warm and sure at the nape of her neck. He stood back, surveying them critically. 'Good. They are heavy and old-fashioned but look well all the same. They are yours now.'

'Mine? But — you do not know if I am the right person. It does not seem right.'

He smiled. 'I gave your rival sapphires. I intend to be fair.'

She said firmly, 'No. I will wear them tonight and then return them to you. If you are able to believe I should be your wife, of course I will accept them. But not yet.'

He bowed his head briefly. 'If that is your wish.'

For the rest of the evening, it seemed Sir Ashton was determined to be charming. He took charge of the conversation but avoided asking the usual trivial questions which could have been difficult for her. Instead, he told her of his own life here and previously, of the death of his grandfather and the qualities of the estate. He gave her opportunities to show interest and ask equally polite questions, and for that she was thankful.

She said, surprised, 'So you are almost a stranger here yourself?'

'Indeed so. My grandfather lived in London, and anyway considered me a nuisance to be provided for, as far away from himself as possible. He intervened very little in my schooling.' He paused. 'Neither to support nor condemn.'

A strange choice of words. She did not like to ask more and he was already saying, 'At least it taught me to look after myself. Until he decided he had need of me and summoned me back.'

She said gently, 'Were you not tempted to refuse?'

He said gravely, 'I would never refuse

to come here, to Ridgeworth. Although at one point, I had almost given up any hope of it. After . . . ' He paused. 'I even thought of beginning a new life overseas. But there was no need for that, fortunately. Besides, my return here has been a restoration in more ways than one. The first house was built by my ancestors. A hundred years or so ago, two branches of the family disagreed — over a will, I believe, and a bitter dispute began. We were ousted from our rightful place; it is only recently that my grandfather regained Ridgeworth.'

'You must have been pleased.'

'I cannot begin to express my satisfaction.' For the first time, there was warmth and passion in his voice. 'I was brought up knowing Ridgeworth should rightfully be mine. And now that it is, there is a great deal to be put right. The last owner was rash and uncaring and my grandfather little better. An estate is a responsibility and my tenants and servants look to me for their livelihood and wellbeing.'

'They will have been reassured by your return.'

'I have seen no evidence of that. Not as yet. I have yet to prove myself. I may be a worse option than my grandfather, for all they know. Indeed, some have already left and I must seek replacements. That reminds me — your rescuer, Haddon tells me he is seeking work; I will give him a trial.'

Surprised, she said, 'Thank you.' It would be comforting to have another familiar face here and pleasing for Mrs Haddon too. But how would Charles manage without him?

Sir Ashton was saying, 'Still, I have hopes that my marriage may engender a significant amount of good feeling here. Everyone loves a wedding, or so I am told. My wife will bring with her joy abounding, and all will end happily as my tenants take her to their hearts, filling her days with kindness and good works and mediating with her villainous husband.'

She raised her eyebrows. 'I believe you are laughing at me.'

'Surely not.'

'And I was ready to believe you.'

He smiled. 'Maybe I am, a little. We shall see. Of course if I were truly a villain, no sane woman would agree to marry me, but would leave on the next passing conveyance with all speed. Fortune or not.' There was a look in his eyes that troubled her.

She said lightly, 'Time will tell. I would hope not to marry a villain, but that is not always apparent before vows are taken. And after that, escape is difficult. Few women have the luxury of making a choice.'

'You are right, of course. It is churlish of me to tease you, in particular when your situation is so difficult.'

The meal was not unduly drawn out. He suggested she should retire early, 'For you have had a tiring day and will be faced with more exertion tomorrow.'

Elinor agreed and withdrew. He had given her a great deal to think about.

She realised that she was beginning to like him, which had to be an advantage. He lacked the easy warmth of Mr Charles, but there was no point in useless regrets. If she could bring Sir Ashton to believe in her, she resolved to fulfil her duties as best she may. And would be grateful for the opportunity fate had offered.

Elinor doubted that she would ever sleep in the vast room she had been given, even in the smaller haven of the four-poster bed. Besides, her head was spinning with new feelings and sensations.

She must have slept, however, for she woke suddenly in darkness. There was someone in the room. She did not know how she knew this. Whatever the sound or movement that had woken her, there was only silence now. She said quietly, 'Mrs Haddon?' She sat up cautiously.

At once a hand was over her mouth while another hand pushed her back down onto the pillows. A harsh voice was close to her ear. 'You're not wanted here. Get out, if you know what's good for you.'

She tried to say through the hand, 'I never wanted to come here. And I have nowhere to go.'

'So find somewhere.' The pillow was jerked from behind her head and pushed onto her face. She could neither see nor breathe. She struggled against the weight and her arms caught in the sheets. As suddenly as the ordeal had begun, the pressure over her face was lifted and she was free. She was gasping and clutching her throat as she tried to recover. The voice said, close to her ear, 'At least ask your intended husband what happened to his first wife.'

Elinor was aware of the door closing. Had he gone? She was shaking now as fear took hold. Had she been dreaming? No, because she could still feel the pressure of his hands against her face and throat. But who could it have been? An intruder? No, someone who had known exactly who she was and why she was here. And clever enough to avoid waking her companion, for Mrs Haddon was snoring peacefully at the foot of the large bed.

What should she do? Elinor lay awake, shivering as she stared into the silent darkness.

In the morning she went down cautiously, ready to view everyone with suspicion. Ashton's 'I trust you slept well?' was met with hesitation and a doubtful look.

'Yes, thank you,' she added belatedly.

'Good. I am pleased to hear it.'

Was he? Or did he know something of what had happened? Was this a devious way of disposing of her and solving his problem? But he needed her to fulfil the stipulation of the will and keep his inheritance. Or did he? Would he prefer the other girl now he had met the two of them? And what was that about a first wife? She shivered.

There were two vehicles waiting outside. Sir Ashton took her elbow and led her to the elegant one standing before the carriage. 'You have no objection to driving with me, I hope?' he asked, smiling. 'Mrs Haddon and Dixon will travel in the coach with the bags.'

A tremor of disquiet shivered through her as she remembered something Charles had said about his recklessness as a whip and a rider, like his father before him. 'With you? Of course not,' she said firmly, hoping her face had not betrayed her doubts. 'Why should I?'

'You will be perfectly safe with me, I can assure you. I will drive as if escorting an elderly aunt.'

She gave him a suspicious glance, feeling that once again laughter lurked behind the grave look. 'I do not feel I care to be compared with an elderly aunt. Please drive however you wish.'

He handed her up onto the seat. 'This will be a new experience for you, I presume.'

So this morning, it seemed, he was willing to put her memories to the test.

She said, 'I expect so.'

They set off sedately enough. He said as they left the estate, 'You will have a better view than you would have had in the carriage.'

'Oh, I see.' She gazed around eagerly at the surroundings and he seemed content to allow her to do so, giving his attention to his team of chestnuts. After the first hour, however, her shoulders slumped a little as her first enthusiasm was turning to disappointment.

He glanced at her face. 'Are you all right? Are you tired?'

'I hoped I might recall this journey. But nothing seems familiar at all.'

'I have to admit, I had hoped so too. But I am hardly surprised.'

She said sharply, 'What do you mean?'

'As far as we know, you have made the journey only once — and it is surprising how different a landscape can be when viewed from the opposite direction. Besides, when we approach our journey's end, you must surely be much more familiar with the country-side.'

She lowered her head. 'I do hope so. You can have no idea how frustrating, and frightening, it is to be forever living as if in a cloud, knowing nothing.'

'It must be. Do not try to force things. I am sure your memory will return.' He paused. 'Am I driving sedately enough for you? I have not frightened you at all?' It was an obvious attempt to change the subject to something more comfortable.

'You are teasing me again. No one could possibly find fault with our pace.'

'You did seem most determined to avoid criticising my driving. Almost as if I have gained an unfortunate reputation. I wonder how?'

She bit her lip. She could not mention Charles and his chance remark but she did not want to lie to him. She said, 'I am not sure how I have gained such an impression. Or even if I have.'

He said, 'I see.'

She hoped he did not. How could she

account for her knowledge?

He continued, 'Perhaps Mrs Haddon said something? My father met his untimely death through driving too recklessly; it is well known. Easy for confusion to arise I suppose.'

'I am sorry — about your father.'

'It was a long time ago.'

'And sorry I have obviously placed too much reliance on local gossip.' She looked away, aware that he was looking at her closely.

It seemed an age before he said calmly, 'No matter.' He turned his attention to the road. She thought unhappily, *He does not believe me*. But what else could she do? She could not confide fully in him when she had made her promise. She sighed. Soon, with the marriage made and obligations fulfilled, she would try to improve Charles's situation, as he so clearly hoped. And then all might be put right between the two men.

She sat for some time, content to admire the adroit way he handled his horses, lightly wielding the long whip. They came to an area of woodland and Sir Ashton slowed to negotiate a bend in the road — and at once, they were surrounded by menacing figures: hats pulled down, dark scarves across their mouths and stout cudgels in hand.

5

Harsh voices were shouting threateningly, although Elinor could not make out what was said.

'Take the whip,' Sir Ashton said. 'Beat them off.'

Somehow she remained calm, obeying without hesitation. Her instincts took over as she brandished the whip with vigour. Beside her, Sir Ashton produced and levelled a pistol and fired. The horses skittered in fright. There were shouts of, 'Arms! Leave them.' And as suddenly as they had appeared, their assailants were gone.

'Did you hit any of them?' Elinor could not believe how steady her voice sounded.

'I fired over their heads.'

'And it had the desired effect.'

'Indeed. Amazingly so. Well, Miss Buckler, travelling with you certainly leads to excitement.'

'I — suppose so. You mean, when I was also attacked on my journey to you? It is fortunate, this time, that you were able to scare them off.'

'Most fortunate.' He added thoughtfully, 'In fact, it was all too easy.'

'Too easy?'

'Were they stupid or merely woefully inefficient? If their intentions had been serious, they could have thrown a couple of logs across the road to halt us and we would have been at their mercy. I could have disposed of one with my pistol and maybe you could have occupied another. The other two could easily have overpowered us. What do you say to that?'

She said briskly, 'That it was a cowardly attack and when they met with any resistance, they lost heart.'

'No doubt. We had better proceed if you are recovered. Although I can guarantee that they will not return.' He smiled. 'You handled that whip well in our defence. I would not wish to have you against me.'

'Thank you. And I am ready to continue.' It was not entirely true. Only now did she realise that her arms were shaking. She pressed them into her sides, hoping Sir Ashton would not notice.

Only as they reached Salisbury did she begin to feel more composed. And now the strangeness of Sir Ashton's words occurred to her for the first time. She thought, *It is as if he does not trust me. Or not wholly.* And he had not seemed surprised. As if he had expected the incident to happen. Elinor was beginning to wonder whether *she* could trust *him*.

He said little more until they were rattling into the city itself. She looked in every direction, hoping to find familiar sights. But now they were pulling into the yard of what must be one of the most fashionable inns, with imposing stonework and pillared doorways. There was noise and bustle as ostlers ran to the horses and she was helped down and ushered inside.

Ashton said, 'The carriage will not be too far behind us, with Mrs Haddon and Dixon. While I check my horses are being well attended, the landlady will show you to your room. Then we will seek out the Reverend Greenwood as soon as we may.'

'Oh, yes. Certainly.'

He smiled grimly. 'The sooner we have this unsatisfactory situation resolved, the better. For both of us. Our destination is within walking distance. A pleasant stroll, no more.'

Elinor hurried to wash her hands and neaten her hair and was ready to leave as Mrs Haddon arrived. Also, she had taken the opportunity to glance once more at the clergyman's affidavit, frowning a little. But there was no chance to voice her doubts until they were embarked upon Sir Ashton's 'pleasant stroll'. As they walked, she ventured, 'Do you know Salisbury well?'

'Hardly at all. Come, we will turn

here. Culver Street. It is not out of our way to St Martin's.'

As they turned the corner, she could not prevent a gasp, quickly suppressed. She hoped Sir Ashton had not noticed her lapse. Surely that had been a familiar figure, disappearing through an archway ahead of them? It had looked, yes, remarkably like Charles. But how could it be?

'Is something wrong?' Sir Ashton was regarding her keenly.

'No. I thought I saw someone I might have recognised — but I believe I must have imagined it. I am sorry.' This would not do. She must be more careful or she would be blurting something out.

Unsettled by the experience, she barely glanced at the ordinary street, lined with cramped houses, their doorways fronting onto the thorough-fare. 'St Martin's? How do you know to go there? The Reverend Greenwood stated I was baptised at Laverstock. Presumably his living is in that parish.'

He stopped, looking directly into her eyes. She stared back as if mesmerised. He said softly, 'And how did I know to take this street?'

'I — do not know.'

'Look around you.'

'Yes. What do you wish me to see?'

'It is where you were living when my agent first discovered you. When you gasped as you did, I hoped you recognised the street. Rather than a person.'

'Oh.' She turned and looked intently at the shabby doors and small windows. 'I do not remember.' She could have wept with the disappointment.

'Apparently you were living at this one.'

She stared at it. 'Surely — if that is so, I should remember? I cannot believe I do not.'

He shrugged. 'Well, no matter. It was probably to be expected. However, the location of this address accounts for my choice of church. This house is within the ancient parish of St Martin. It would seem a likely conclusion.'

'Yes.' She was feeling more hopeful. It was more important to find someone who knew her. There was no real need for her memory to be regained so quickly, although she would be unbelievably glad when it did.

They arrived at the vicarage within minutes as Sir Ashton had promised. Ushered inside by the maidservant, Elinor gazed at the elderly cleric, desperate to recognise him. Worse than her own lack of response, however, was the blank politeness with which the vicar was regarding her. 'I am sorry,' he said, as Sir Ashton explained the situation. 'I am afraid I cannot help you. If this young woman lived within this parish, I do not recollect her ever attending my services.'

'And you will know all your parishioners by sight, naturally. I congratulate you, Reverend. Although a congregation of a small and select nature might allow that.'

The man gave a smug smile. 'On the

contrary, my services are exceedingly well attended. But during my sermons, I make a point of fixing my eyes upon the faces below me. How else are my flock to take my words to heart and benefit from my preaching?'

'Quite.' Sir Ashton's tone was cold.

'Although of course, individuals are not bound to attend within their own parish. They are at liberty to go to any church they wish. However, I flatter myself they will not receive better sermonizing within the cathedral itself.' The vicar was warming to his theme.

'We are sorry to have troubled you,' Elinor said quickly. 'Could you perhaps tell us where we may find the Reverend Greenwood? Here, see.'

The vicar scanned the paper in a perfunctory manner. 'I am not familiar with the name. And I know little of Laverstock anyway, that being a rustic parish outside the city.' He gave the impression that the surrounding villages were beneath his notice. 'The bishop of course would be familiar with all the incumbents and might be found in the Cathedral Close, he added.

Sir Ashton strode so quickly through the churchyard that Elinor could hardly keep up. 'Slowly, Sir Ashton, please. I cannot get my breath.'

He paused then. 'Insufferable man. If you had lived next door to the church, I could well understand your walking three miles or more to avoid his sermons — and the prospect of sitting with his stern gaze fixed upon you and urging repentance.'

In spite of her disappointment, Elinor laughed. 'So we are to follow his suggestion?'

'I will send a boy with a note to the bishop. We will return to the inn for some refreshment.'

At last it seemed that Sir Ashton's enquiries were to meet with success. A note was written, and a reliable boy found and dispatched. Scarcely had they finished the light repast provided by the innkeeper, when they were rewarded by a visitor asking for Sir

Ashton by name.

Another clerical gentleman — but this one could not have been more different, smiling helpfully from the first. 'My lord, I have heard that you have been asking for me. I regret exceedingly that you have had so much trouble. I am the Reverend Greenwood, of the parish of Laverstock, at your service.'

Sir Ashton nodded. 'It was good of you to come, and so promptly.'

'By great good fortune I had business with the bishop, and so am at hand for you. And so, how may I be of assistance? Ah.' As if only now he had noticed Elinor. 'Miss Buckler! How are you faring? Of course, you have come to ask me to verify the affidavit I signed for you.'

'You know who I am?' At last! Elinor could hardly believe it.

He frowned, the frown disturbing the round and affable face only briefly. 'Why should I not? I have known you from a child. Until your change in financial circumstances when, despite my best efforts, your rented cottage was lost to you and you moved into the city with your mother, who sadly died soon afterwards. Of course, you had hardly been within the city a matter of weeks before you were blessed with your good fortune. You were discovered by the efficient young man representing Sir Ashton here.' He bowed.

She said, 'Thank you for all you have done.' The words were hardly adequate for such enthusiasm and good will, even though nothing he mentioned struck any chord with her. And yet why did she not feel more liking for this effusive cleric? It was hardly his fault if his manner was excessive and his smile seemed to lack genuine warmth. She was being churlish and ungrateful.

It was as if he read her thoughts. He said, 'But what is this? Something is not right, I feel.' He was glancing from one to the other. 'Do you not recognise me?'

'Miss Buckler has met with an

unfortunate accident,' Sir Ashton said. 'During her journey to my house. She cannot recall who she is — or any of the details you have so usefully verified. So you see, your affidavit and testimony are essential.'

The Reverend Greenwood shook his head sorrowfully. 'Indeed. How terrible. But how fortunate that I am here, as you so kindly remark. I can vouch most strongly for Miss Buckler and there is no problem in the proof of her identity. I am glad everything is so easily resolved. If there is anything I can do further, you must not hesitate to summon me at any time. I insist.'

Small risk of that, Elinor thought wryly. She murmured, 'That is most kind. You have put my mind at rest.' She wanted nothing more than to be rid of him. 'I cannot think of anything else. Thank you.'

'Yes,' Sir Ashton said suddenly. 'There is. You can marry us. At once.'

Elinor stared at him. Her shock and surprise were mirrored, she knew, in the clergyman's face. She said, 'You mean — straightaway, my lord?'

'Certainly,' Sir Ashton said pleasantly. 'I see no reason to delay.'

'No, of course. Why should there be? But — do not the banns have to be called?'

'Not at all. I have had a special licence in readiness since I first heard that you had been found.'

Elinor said stupidly, 'But you have only just met me.'

'I knew your name. I had a small difficulty at one point of having an over-abundance of young ladies claiming that name — but I merely had to decide who was the most convincing claimant. Obviously I have now chosen you.'

'That is most kind.' Keeping her voice steady proved difficult. 'But what about — the other? What will happen when she returns? What will she say?'

'We shall await that with interest, I have no doubt.'

The Reverend Greenwood was on his

feet, bowing. He seemed to have recovered a little from his surprise and a measure of colour was returning to his face. 'Well, my lord, if you wish there to be no delay, I will leave for the church immediately.'

'Thank you. Most kind. But please do travel with us.'

'I rode here; I will be quicker alone. And if I arrive first, I shall be ready to meet you attired appropriately and with everything needful prepared, so that there will be at least some ceremony to the occasion. As befits such a beautiful bride.'

Sir Ashton smiled. 'That is almost a rebuke, I fear. You consider me too hasty.'

'No, of course not. I would not be so presumptuous. Witnesses, my lord. Do you have your own or do you wish me to find some? The vergers will oblige if necessary.'

'I am sure they would. We will have our own, however — the worthy Mr and Mrs Haddon.'

As the vicar left hurriedly, Elinor too recovered herself, not certain that she welcomed such high-handedness. 'Is there such a need for haste?'

'I think so. I would rather you did not disagree with me on this.' His voice was deceptively mild. She supposed in her difficult situation, it should hardly matter. And was not this what she had wanted? Yet suddenly she had had her fill of being swept along by the wishes of others. Even dear Charles had made certain that she should follow his suggestions. She said, 'I have nothing suitable to wear.'

'You look well enough to me.'

'But this is my wedding day.'

He nodded. 'So it would seem. Well, we shall inform the Haddons and then be on our way to the parish of Laverstock.' He had taken no notice of her protest at all. He added, 'I believe the good reverend has had a fair start.'

What a strange turn of phrase, Elinor thought crossly. Almost as if Sir Ashton considered this to be a child's game of hide-and-seek. Sir Ashton was instructing Haddon to take the carriage. 'Thus we shall have our witnesses with us. All ordered and correct, as required.'

As they drove out of the city to the north, however, he told Haddon to stop and threw a coin to a girl selling flowers. He turned to Elinor. 'So — now my bride has a posy, at least.'

'Oh. Thank you.' He had taken account of her feelings after all. She hid her confusion by lifting the violets to her face.

He said quietly, 'But you do not need violets. You outdo them. Never think otherwise.'

She stared at him. Was he being serious this time? Or merely paying a compliment to suit the occasion? But he did not seem a man to deal in empty sentiments.

The village of Laverstock was not far, straggling along the dusty road. They pulled up outside the church and began to walk along the path, Sir Ashton taking her arm and Mr and Mrs

Haddon following behind. Only on reaching the porch did they see that the door was closed. Silently, Sir Ashton pushed it open. The church was empty.

Elinor said, 'But I do not understand! Where is the Reverend Greenwood?'

'Perhaps we should seek him in the vicarage,' Sir Ashton said easily.

'Yes, of course. Perhaps his preparations are taking longer than he expected. Or perhaps he has been waylaid by a needy parishioner.'

'Perhaps.'

Within a very few moments, they had taken the path to the side of the church and Sir Ashton was ringing the bell. The door was opened by a woman who bobbed hastily at the sight of such illustrious visitors but was rapidly perplexed. 'There must be some mistake, I am afraid, sir. There is no Reverend Greenwood here and never has been. The vicar is away from home at present; he has been at a sickbed all day. Would you care to come in and wait? I could send a boy with a message.'

'No need for that. We are sorry to have troubled you.'

They retreated, Elinor hardly able to contain her feelings. 'What is happening? Where is the Reverend Greenwood?'

'I suspect we have seen the last of him.' Sir Ashton did not seem at all disconcerted by this.

'You knew! You never expected to meet him here.'

Sir Ashton looked at her, raising his eyebrows. 'And you did not know?'

'What? Of course not. How could I?'

'Well, there is a question, certainly.'

'I do not understand you.' She was adrift all over again and more lost than ever. The small certainties she had been able to build within her new life were tumbled about her feet like a child's toy tower of bricks. She must begin again. She tried to make sense of it, talking partly as if to herself. 'The Reverend Greenwood is obviously not known here — and yet he particularly said he was from Laverstock, which is where the affidavit states I was born. Could there be another village of that name nearby?'

'There is not.'

'No, I suppose there would not be. You will have checked that at the inn. And it is an unusual name. But the Reverend Greenwood recognised me. Or he said he did. And he sought us out.'

'So he did.'

'So he had heard of our search and knew who he would find.' She sighed. 'It seemed so convenient when he appeared, ready to be so obliging.'

'I thought so myself.'

She pressed her fingers to her eyes, knowing she could easily have wept. 'He was the proof of my identity — and he has gone. Why would he do that?'

'Presumably because he was not the vicar of Laverstock. Or even the Reverend Greenwood. Or even a member of the clergy at all. Well done, my dear. Your acting talents are most impressive. I could swear that you are genuinely shocked and upset.'

'I am. What I am is how I seem. I have told you nothing but the truth.' She was striving to keep her temper.

'Maybe so.' He spoke in a cool and level tone. 'But I suspect you are not telling me the whole truth.'

Heat rushed to her face and the denial died on her lips. But how had she betrayed herself? How could he know about Charles? She longed to confide in Sir Ashton but it was too soon. It would ruin everything and she must keep her promise. She said in a low voice, 'There is nothing more I can tell you.'

There was a short silence while it seemed that Sir Ashton was waiting to see if she might think of something else. He said at last, 'Well, let us return to the inn and thus to Ridgeworth. It seems your affidavit is worth little, which is most unfortunate. Still, all this is most pleasing from my point of view. It can only enhance my good opinion of myself to have two such charming applicants who will stop at nothing to marry me.'

'I will not hold you to anything, Sir Ashton,' she flashed.

'Perhaps there will be more applicants?' he continued as if she had not spoken. 'I am like a princess of old in a golden tower. Perhaps I should set impossible tasks which can only be completed by the rightful bride. What is usual? Passing silken dresses through gold rings is frequently done, I believe.'

She found herself smiling. 'I do not believe I possess that skill.'

'As I said, we shall return to the house tomorrow and consider what to do next. Do not worry; I am determined to unravel this mystery, one way or another.'

'I sincerely hope that you may.'

Throughout the return journey to the inn, they were both silent. Elinor was going through the morning's surprising events in her mind, trying to make sense of them. Why had the fake reverend practised his deceit? What had he hoped to gain? Or perhaps he been acting upon someone else's instructions. If so, someone who had Elinor's interests at heart. Because this must have been intended to prove her the real Miss Elinor Buckler, since she was unable to provide any proof herself.

Sir Ashton gave instructions for Elinor to have refreshment in her room, once again to be ready for an early start. She was thankful, being too weary and confused for polite conversation. She ate little, wanting only to sleep — but once in bed was wide awake as her thoughts allowed her no rest. Every time she closed her eyes, Charles's care and concern vied with Sir Ashton's obvious mistrust. And there was the attack in the woods — and the sinister warning she had been given at Ridgeworth.

She tossed and turned and dozed restlessly, to awake at last, suddenly, before it was entirely light — and knowing what she must do. She would leave, and at once. Whatever the truth of it, her position was unbearable. She would decide what to do next when her memory returned and until then, both men must wait: Mr Charles Buckler for the restitution of what was due to him, and Sir Ashton for the opportunity to fulfil his promise to his grandfather.

6

Sir Ashton also woke with a new sense of resolution and with a clear course of action revealed to him. He knew now he did not believe Elinor, or not entirely, and also knew he did not care.

Yesterday, in the city, she had glimpsed and recognised Charles, disappearing around a distant corner. Ashton was certain of it. His old enemy was someone he would never mistake, even at a distance. But the way Elinor had known him too, and pretended otherwise, hit him hard, with a great blow of sorrow and anguish. He was surprised at himself. He had only just met the girl but she had become important to him. It would have been sensible to challenge her at once, but he said nothing. Unmasking her would have meant she must be packed off and given up. He could not do that.

It was no surprise to him that when the Reverend Greenwood appeared so conveniently, he could be so soon defeated. Ashton smiled with amusement at the way he had called the man's bluff. But in spite of his harsh words and the need to put Elinor into that difficult situation merely to observe her reactions, he was still disposed to think well of her. She would hardly be the first person to be deceived and manipulated by Charles and his family.

As yet there was no sign of Elinor, but yesterday had been a day of unpleasant shocks. No doubt she was still weary. He was driving her too hard — but it could not be helped. They must make their way through this maze and discover the truth one way or another. Elinor might be withholding part of the truth, but the first girl had lied about the whole of it; he was certain of that.

He had eaten the ham and eggs set before him without noticing, deep in thought. Where was she? He was on his feet looking at his watch when he heard hurried footsteps on the stairs. Good. They would not be too late in leaving after all.

There was a tap on the parlour door and Mrs Haddon was before him, wringing her hands together. 'Oh, sir! I am sorry. I do not understand it. She has gone.'

He stared at her. 'Gone? How can this be?'

'I am so sorry, Sir Ashton. I heard nothing. When I woke Miss Elinor seemed to be still asleep, and I thought after the trials of yesterday to give her a little more time.'

He raised his eyebrows. 'Go on.'

'I opened the curtains but she did not stir, and then I realised she wasn't in the bed as I thought but only a pillow, lengthwise, with the bedding arranged round it.'

Again, he felt as if he had been struck a blow. His first thought was that the woman must be mistaken, he must check the room — but of course there could be no mistake. And he could not, must not, lose her. He cut across Mrs Haddon's well-meaning ramblings. 'Where could she have gone? Have you any idea?'

'No, I do not. Oh, Sir Ashton, if I did I would say. I hope she doesn't come to harm. She is such a sweet lady.'

He was thinking furiously. Elinor knew this city. Or would if she could remember it. Had she recognised some part of her surroundings yesterday after all? He could have sworn she had not. But there had been that glimpse of Charles. Would she have known where to find him and gone to him, somehow? The pain of that thought pierced his heart. No, he was being too fanciful, thinking he saw Charles at every turn, still haunted by all that lay between them. And why would Elinor know of him?

Perhaps her memory had returned in the night and she had decided she would have none of Sir Ashton after all. But even so, where would she go? His agent had been quite clear about it: she had no one, nothing. He groaned. Even so, she had chosen to take her chance with poverty and loneliness, rather than endure him. Knowing what he knew, he could hardly blame her.

*   *   *

Dawn was hardly breaking as Elinor had slipped away and set off, knowing what she must do. She made her way back to Culver Street, which was easily found. Yesterday she had been so disappointed at being confronted with this street and finding it unfamiliar that she had failed to suggest the obvious steps they should have taken. Of course, at the time, she had been placing all her hopes upon the false Reverend Greenwood. So Culver Street had seemed merely a distraction. And Sir Ashton presumably had not needed to make further enquiries there; his agent would have done that. He would have reported back when he discovered her and waited for further instructions before approaching her, or so she supposed. But why had Sir Ashton failed to ask whether anyone living on the street recognised her?

Working people were stirring already. No one looked twice at her as she knocked several times before a woman of middle years opened the door, wiping her fingers on a greasy apron and looking down at her hands.

Elinor said, 'You have rooms here, I believe?'

'I did but they're taken. Sorry.' The woman made as if to step back. Elinor put out a hand to stay her and the woman looked directly into her face for the first time. 'Bless me! It's Miss Buckler. I didn't think to see you back again. But what's happened? Why are you here?'

Elinor could have fainted with the relief of it. She took some deep breaths and steadied herself on the doorpost. 'You recognise me?'

'Well, of course I do. How could I

forget it? Otherwise, I admit I might not, since you were with me for so short a time. But come in and rest. You don't look well. Whatever can have happened? So pale and ill-looking as you are, and I thought you'd fallen on your feet and no mistake. But you never can tell, can you?'

In spite of the lack of sleep and not many days having gone by since her accident, Elinor had until now felt capable of doing what she intended. But being assured of how weak and ill she looked had a negative effect. She clenched her fingers, determined to be strong, but her body swayed treacherously and she found herself supported firmly and taken into a back room, warm with the heat of the stove and cooking pots. She was pressed gently down onto a stool and offered a cup full of something warm. Some kind of broth. Best not to think about it too closely. She sipped it gratefully.

'So what was it? What happened?' Her hostess pulled up another stool and sat down herself, leaning forward, obviously not wanting to miss the slightest word or glance.

Elinor tried to gather her thoughts but she was beginning to feel drowsy. She had hoped the broth would revive her but it seemed to be having the opposite effect. She said, 'So much has happened.' Her words did not sound as they should.

'It did not turn out as you had hoped, is that it? Your fine gentleman did not intend marriage after all? I have to say, I did wonder; it seemed too good to be true. But it wasn't my place to advise you against it.'

'No, not that. It seems, I am told, an accident. On the journey. Was left for dead — but before that I cannot remember anything.' She stifled a yawn.

The woman sat back, mouth open with amazement. 'What, nothing at all? You mean, you do not know any of it? So, let me see . . . surely you must know who you are? And remember living here?' She shook her head as

Elinor was doing the same. 'You do not! My goodness me, I never heard of such a thing.' Her voice seemed to be coming from a great distance. 'I am Betsey Brockway, my dear. At your service.'

Elinor tried to reply but her mouth would not obey her. She flopped backwards and strong hands caught her and propped her up against the wall. Footsteps entering the room. Male voices. Betsey Brockway asking about a cart. Wrapping a greasy, threadbare blanket closely around her head and shoulders. Elinor tried to pull away from the confining wool but could not move her arms. What was happening? What were they going to do to her? She wanted to scream but could not. She was in a wordless, helpless world where she was completely in the power of these strangers. She was trapped.

★ ★ ★

'Good,' someone said briskly. Another voice entirely. 'You're awake at last. I was thinking there would be another night wasted.'

There was a bitter taste in Elinor's mouth and her head was aching. But at least she could move her limbs. The woman who had spoken was pulling her into a sitting position. 'You had been long enough getting here as it was. I knew you'd not thank me for letting you sleep. You will be wanting to begin.'

She was in a small but fashionable room. She gained an impression of mirrors and crimson and white stripes, overdone rather than tasteful. She said, 'To begin?'

'Indeed, yes. Your new life. And full of promise it will be too, if you play your cards well.'

'But — I have a life. I am Elinor Buckler, lately living in Salisbury. And where is this?'

The woman shook her head. 'Now, then, I don't know what lies you've been told but you've been taken in and no mistake. I've been expecting you, as arranged. Here in London, city of opportunity.'

It was the information Elinor had been hoping for. But she was unable to welcome it. 'So you know who I am?'

'But of course. It is all in the paper that came with you. Verifying what I had already been told by word of mouth.'

Yet another paper. And yet this woman spoke with so much conviction. 'Where is it? May I see it?'

'Can you read?' The woman peered at her as she nodded. 'Well, that is an unusual accomplishment in our line. But might well serve excellently for what we have in mind. Here, I have it safe in my pocket.'

It did not have the official look of the Reverend Greenwood's false affidavit. But the effect of the crumpled paper with an uneven scrawl was convincing. She stared at it: 'I recommend to you Miss Jane Blackett, who I am certain has all the abilities required for a successful career with you in your establishment.'

Another name. Another identity. Jane Blackett. Was there a ring of truth and recognition here at last? She could not tell. Her head was aching too much to decide anything. Her companion reached for the paper, almost snatching it. 'For it is addressed to me, of course.'

'Yes. Of course,' Elinor echoed. 'I have lost my memory. As I am sure you know. But this new name does not seem at all familiar. You are sure there could not be any mistake? And please, excuse me, I do not know who you are.'

The woman bobbed. 'Mrs Diamond, my dear. By name and nature. Mistake? There is no chance of that. The person who sent you does not make mistakes.'

'And I have been sent to you by way of an introduction? But who sent me?' And an introduction to what? But there was no need to ask. Her loss of memory had obviously not robbed her of awareness of the darker side of life. *Please*, she thought, *let me be wrong*. She felt a wave of longing for her identity as Elinor. Why had she been so determined to prove it? Ashton had seemed willing to accept her. Ashton. Would she ever see him again? The sense of loss was hard to bear.

'Ah, I keep my sources to myself. You'll understand that, I'm sure.'

Enveloped in despair, Elinor had almost forgotten her question. How did it matter how she came to be here? She *was* here and must make the best of it. Unless she could find an opportunity to get away. Yes, that was what she must do.

'Come,' Mrs Diamond said. 'Up you get. No time to waste. I have a most suitable dress for you. I must have known.' Elinor was dragged to her feet as the cheery voice continued. Somehow her limbs were pushed and pulled into a garment that to Elinor hardly seemed substantial enough to be called a dress. She tried to adjust her neckline.

'There!' Mrs Diamond stood back a little, her wide smile of satisfaction revealing blackened teeth. 'Modesty and innocence. That's it exactly.'

'Yes. Thank you,' Elinor said faintly. She must make no further mention of mistaken identity. She suspected Mrs Diamond would be unlikely to part with her so easily. Indeed, Elinor's true identity might not matter to her. 'You must forgive me. I have never done anything like this before.' She was hesitating to ask for further details.

'Isn't that the whole purpose? You are far more valuable because of that.' She leered. 'As I am sure you know. Now, we will not have any of the others with us tonight. You will stand alone, the picture of innocent charm. When we arrive, I will show you the wealthy gentlemen who will be your most likely prospects. I have one or two in mind already.'

'And what must I do?'

Mrs Diamond cackled with laughter. 'Bless you! I'm sure you have a gift for it. Simper, just so, and look simple and confused, just as you are doing now. You will be a great hit, mark my words.'

'And where are we going?'

'Why, to Drury Lane, to the theatre. Don't worry, I shall be near at hand at all times.'

Elinor felt a stirring of hope. Perhaps she could slip away in the crowded streets or around the theatre itself.

However, any prospect of escape on the way was quashed as soon as they left the house, which seemed to be shabby but respectable enough. Not only was Mrs Diamond clutching her arm tightly, but at once they were joined by a couple of menservants with cudgels. She glanced at the face of the one nearest to her, hoping for the slightest sign of kindliness, but saw a grim visage with a crooked nose and old scars. The men were busy pushing a way through the crush of bodies for them but would be swift to catch her if she even tried to slip away.

At least the coldness of the night air was clearing her head. She must not give way to despair but she could see no way out of this. *And*, she thought miserably, *if I truly am Jane Blackett, who was obviously happy enough to accept this kind of life, what then? Must I find a wealthy patron and make the best of things, no doubt making a generous payment to Mrs Diamond along the way? Surely I would have to be desperate to have ever considered that course. And now I have met Ashton, I do not believe I can.*

* * *

Ashton knew where he must begin his search. Why had he not taken this course yesterday? he berated himself. Because of course Granger had spoken to the landlady already. And he had expected the vicar of the parish to recognise her. And most of all, seeing Charles and witnessing Elinor's reaction to him and her denial had profoundly unsettled him.

His omission would be rectified now. This would be where Elinor had begun, since he had helpfully shown her the street and the house. He knocked on the door sharply, to have it opened almost at once by a thin, sharp-featured, hurried woman. She had one hand already outstretched. 'I did what — ' she began. 'Oh. Sorry, sir. I mistook you.'

'So it seems. May I come in?'

'Yes. Yes, of course.' She stepped back — reluctantly, he thought. 'All the rooms are for the lodgers, sir. There's only the kitchen to sit in.'

'No matter. I am no stranger to kitchens.' He smiled at her but she seemed more worried than ever. 'This way?' He walked down the narrow passage towards the back of the house without waiting for an answer.

'You must excuse the state of it, sir. I was called out unexpectedly, early this morning. To my sick sister.'

'I am sorry to hear that. Nothing too serious I hope, since you are already returned?'

'Serious? Ah, no. Thank you, sir.'

Ashton raised his eyebrows, not

convinced. 'Good. I am enquiring about a young woman who may have called here this morning. She used to have lodgings here.'

She said, too quickly, 'I'm sorry but as I told you, I wasn't here. I've seen no young women.'

'And the other people here? Might your lodgers have seen her?'

'All out by now. I only take people who are gainfully employed.'

'But I believe this young lady worked from this house itself, with her needle. No one else does the same?'

A rapid shake of the head.

'Maybe you at least remember Miss Elinor Buckler when she lived here?'

The woman hesitated. She was obviously so nervous now that she was no longer certain what she could safely say, he thought. She said, 'Yes, I believe so. People come and go so quickly.'

He said more gently, 'There is nothing to fear in telling the truth.'

'Yes, sir. I didn't realise at first who you meant, being as I knew her as Nell, as her mother called her. She lived here for a number of weeks, with her mother, until that lady died. But that was no fault of mine. They were very comfortable here. The older lady was ill when she came.' She repeated everything Granger had already discovered; her account tallied with his. However, she would not budge from her statement that she had not seen Elinor since. And he was certain she was not telling him everything she knew. Not even when he offered her a guinea for any further information. By the look in her eyes she wanted to take it, but still she shook her head.

'If you should recall anything, I will leave you my direction,' he said pleasantly. Someone, he thought, had made a very good job of closing her mouth. Charles, maybe?

He turned away from the door as it closed behind him and regarded the neighbouring houses. There was little else he could do. There, the occupants were much more eager to be helpful, particularly at the mention of a possible reward. Even to the extent of inventing a young lady with fair hair and a blue dress. He shook his head. This was all taking too long. He was almost certain she must have come here — but had she left willingly, or not?

'Sir?' The door had opened again. He smiled grimly. So the promise of payment had worked after all. 'I was thinking, she may have taken the Shaftesbury road. She wanted to know where she came from. I told her Donhead St Mary, off the Shaftesbury road.'

'Thank you.' He filled the outstretched palm. Something at last. And yet, he had a feeling of unease which he could not pin down.

'Sir.' He turned back to the door but she had gone. This voice had come from the other side of the street. Looking round, he saw a thin, small boy who seemed familiar in some way. 'If you're asking after that lady you was with yesterday . . . '

Of course. This was the boy he had sent to the bishop when they had been seeking the Reverend Greenwood. 'I may be at that.'

'I saw her come here this morning. No mistake. I followed her because it was so early and I thought there might be more messages for me to take.'

'And? What then?' His voice was urgent. 'Where did she go?'

'I don't know if I saw her come out. She went inside, for some time. And then a closed cart came up to the door with two men in it. They went in too, and then I couldn't see rightly but they seemed to bring somebody out, all wrapped in a big shawl. Almost carrying her, it looked like.'

He was angered and encouraged simultaneously. Or was the boy imagining this in his eagerness to please? 'Did you follow this cart?'

'Yes, until they left the city and took the London road.'

'London? You're sure of that? Not Shaftesbury?'

'No. I know the London road, sir. But then I thought I should come back and see you. But you weren't at the inn, so finding you took longer.'

'No matter.' He considered this swiftly. To begin with, no clues at all as to where Elinor might have gone; and now two possibilities. He could not afford to miss following either of them. Yes, he knew what must be done. Dixon must take the Shaftesbury road and Ashton would follow the trail to London.

7

It would be easy, Ashton had thought, for Dixon to discover whether Elinor was on the road to the west. So he had hoped the other man would have rejoined him before he reached London, but unfortunately there was no sign of him. A pity, because Ashton could have made good use of him now.

Dixon had known the poorer districts well. Since the day of Ashton's coming to his aid in a street fight they had established a firm bond, sharing lodgings and resources. He had often wondered what instinct had made him pitch in, but had never regretted it. The two young men had lived on their wits. Dixon never spoke of his background, although Ashton had the impression he had not always been poor; while Ashton's grandfather had made it clear he must manage alone.

Would Sophia have married him if she had known his true circumstances from the first? But she was stubborn and had loved him. He frowned. *Do not think about that*. He had lost one wife; he would not lose Elinor.

His search had begun well. The two men and the cart described to him had left sour memories on their road, through their surly reluctance to speak to anyone. And once arrived in London, even without Dixon, he had not lost the ability to question discreetly without causing alarm. One or two old acquaintances were still frequenting the Sun and Lantern inn and were pleased to report back to him. He must at all times conceal his anxiety and frustration at what might be happening to Elinor while his progress seemed so slow. At last, however, he had come to the house in a shabbily unremarkable street not far from Covent Garden.

He regarded the front door from across the road. From what he had gathered from his contacts, girls came here willingly. Of its kind, Mrs Diamond's establishment was well-regarded. She did not need to stoop to drugging and intimidating young servant girls fresh from the country, as so often happened. But that did not mean she would never agree to such practices if the reward was high enough.

The door opened and instinctively he stepped back, although the people emerging took no notice of him. She was there. Elinor herself. With an elderly woman in a black cloak and rusty bonnet. Hope and joy surged within him. He was waiting only for the street to clear of vehicles before striding across to reclaim her. No, wait. Now he observed the strong-armed escort; he hesitated to tackle them alone. And Elinor might be harmed in the resulting fight. Besides, whatever had happened to her in Salisbury, she had left his company of her own free will.

But she was not going to stay here with that woman; he was determined of that. He would have to try something else. He set out to follow the small party, his heart feeling as if it was gripped with an iron-cold vice.

* * *

Trying to seem at ease with the situation, Elinor ventured, 'Which play are we to see?'

Mrs Diamond laughed. 'We don't trouble ourselves with the play. There will be far more action off the stage than on it, and a great deal more profitable. No, we are going to the lobby. You'll see.'

If Elinor had thought the street crowded, the theatre lobby with such a press of bodies and filled with shrill voices and laughter clouded her head yet again. So many young women in bright and flimsy garments; and thankfully, her dress was indeed modest in comparison. Women with scarlet feathers in their hair and azure ribbons, smiling lips and blank eyes. Close to, many were older than they appeared. Wealthy men strolled and fumbled amongst them, making lewd comments. It was hot, airless and overwhelming. She thought, *I must not faint. Not here.* Heaven knew where she might wake if she did.

A young man with a long nose and a cruel mouth leered at her as he edged towards them.

'Not him,' Mrs Diamond said in her ear. 'In debt up to the armpits. Not that any of them are strangers to credit, but we deal only in hard gold. You must remember that, dear.' She was pulling Elinor away. 'I wouldn't normally do this; you're better seeking them out on your own. But being your first time, I shall show you how to go on. Ah! That's better. In the old-fashioned dark hat, over by the mirrors.'

'That old man?' Elinor whispered.

'Never call any of them old. You are their regained youth, never forget that. And age equals money, as like as not. There, see. He's looking over at you.

Smile back but drop your chin shyly. That's right. Now glance up. That's perfect. He's coming.'

Elinor did as she was told, her heart beating too fast. He was close enough now for her to see watering eyes and a running nose. Presumably he and Mrs Diamond would be making some financial arrangement. She kept her eyes to her feet, thinking fast. Where would he take her? Once outside, or even in some quiet corner, maybe she could break away from him. He did not seem too steady on his feet. Surely she could outrun him? Unless the two guards were to follow them. Her heart sank. They would, of course. Mrs Diamond was no fool.

A strong but subtle moving of the figures before her. The old man said indignantly, 'You pushed me aside, sir.'

A familiar voice answered him. 'My pardon, sir. But this lady is spoken for.'

Ashton! And now she almost did faint, swaying with relief. She looked up at him, eyes smiling her joy. His face was polite but implacable. Mrs Diamond said, 'By whom? And she is expensive.'

'So I should hope.' He seized Elinor's hand, thrust a bulging purse into Mrs Diamond's palm and was pulling Elinor away. Dimly, Elinor was aware of the old man's protests and Mrs Diamond's soothing tones as they were out of the crowd, through the door and down the wide shallow steps.

Were they safe? Elinor could hardly believe the joyous shock of it. 'Will they come after us?'

'Those two bully boys? Let them try. I have brought my own.'

Behind them, she was aware of a fight breaking out. There was a harsh note to Ashton's laughter as he said, 'My two will keep them busy for a while. That's all that's needed until Mother Diamond calls them off.'

'You know her?'

'I know of her. But she will expect that payment to be repeated, many times no doubt. Whereas to my mind, she has been lucky to receive that. Are you able to walk far?' He was supporting her with his arm. Her legs were aching and she felt weak. But she must go on. Under no account would she hinder her rescuer. Ashton held out a hand to a passing cab and helped her up.

'Are we safe now?'

'We soon will be. I am having no more of this.' His voice was grim. 'I want the legal right to protect you and no one will prevent me.' He smiled, taking the sting from his words. 'Even you.'

'I am so sorry. I know where my folly almost led me.' She shuddered. 'I only wanted to know who I am. Beyond doubt. To have the proof.'

'I too, but that can come later.' He tapped on the roof. 'Here.'

She had hoped they would travel further. How could they be safe already? But she must trust his judgement. Quickly, his arms around her shoulders, he was ushering her inside a dark building. Yet another church. Of course. And a cleric who bowed his head and whose hands shook but seemed to know what he was about. Witnesses who were unknown to her, and she would surmise were also unknown to Ashton, but would serve their purpose.

Ashton kept one arm around her, supporting her, and with his other hand slipped a ring upon her finger. She recited the required words as if in a dream. Ashton was leading her back down the aisle. He said calmly, 'At last. This is not what I would have chosen for you, but that can be put right later. Never fear, you shall have the ceremony you deserve. But for now you are, as my wife, a great deal safer. I have the right to protect you.'

In spite of it all, Elinor was aware of a deep-running joy in the depths of her being. She loved him. All that she wanted was to be his wife. And Ashton? Surely he must feel something for her to wish to protect her — and might grow to love her too.

Another hackney took them to a small inn to the west of the city. He smiled for the first time. 'It is at least fairly clean and the landlord is an old friend. And Dixon will know where to find us.'

She could hardly stay awake; was only aware having his arms around her and falling into a deep slumber as soon as her head touched the pillows. She awoke suddenly, alert at once and remembering everything. Knowing disappointment that he was no longer beside her. He was up and about before her, if he had slept at all. Brisk and businesslike. 'It seems that I spend a great deal of time finding dresses for you.' He was smiling. 'Here, this will be more suitable for travelling.'

'Thank you.' She never wished to see the other again. She was up and dressed and finishing a light breakfast when Dixon arrived.

Ashton's face lightened at the sight of him. He clapped Dixon on the shoulder. 'It's good to see you. And you may wish us happy. We are man and wife.'

If Dixon was surprised, he concealed it well. He nodded. 'I'm disappointed to have missed it. To stand as your witness if nothing else, with you lacking a brother.'

'None else I would rather have. Friend, brother, all of those. You know that. But not knowing who abducted Elinor and who my enemies are, I could not take the risk of delay.'

'Of course.' Dixon paused. 'I could make a suggestion as to that. I was followed here.'

Ashton's eyes narrowed. 'Were you, now? And by — ?'

'Mr Charles Buckler — your predecessor, and a ready enemy more than any, I would say.'

They were not looking at Elinor. She opened her mouth and closed it again. Should she speak out in his defence? Yes, she was safely married now — but surely it was too soon. She was hardly in the position of strength Charles had suggested. But how could she allow them to think so wrongly of him?

Ashton was saying, 'Why would he seek to prevent my marriage?'

Dixon shrugged. 'General malevolence? Because the marriage was what your grandfather wanted?'

'Maybe. Thank you for the warning.' Ashton grinned. 'And you allowed him to follow you?'

'I made certain of it. So I could know where he was. Less of a problem that way.'

'And where is he now?'

Dixon was naming another inn; a street and district that meant nothing to Elinor. 'I have someone keeping a watch on him. If he should try anything untoward, I'll know of it.'

That could do no harm, Elinor thought uneasily. Unless Charles had realised she had been taken and was searching for her. In that case, he must keep away. Could she warn him somehow?

Ashton said, 'I should have kept you with me instead of sending you off towards Shaftesbury.'

'You weren't to know that. They knew of her in that village, by the way. Knew of an Elinor Buckler at any rate. And you seem to have managed pretty well without me.'

'There's more to be done. I've employed Burns and Bradby as protection and they've done well. I shall employ them to escort us back.'

'You won't go far wrong with those two.'

'But I want you to stay here. Only a day or two at most, but to see if you can find out anything further about my wife's abduction. If Charles was at the root of it I want to know. But discreetly. Take care not to warn him off. Not yet.'

Elinor felt that if she did not speak she would burst. It could not be Charles. Yes, he had a plan that involved her, but this was so far from the truth that it was almost laughable. Ah, but this would all be for the best. If Dixon

135

could find out who had done it, Charles would be cleared. She smiled at Dixon. 'Thank you.'

He looked at her directly for the first time — a piercing gaze that held her transfixed. 'Don't thank me until I've achieved something.' He smiled back and the dark, stern face lightened. 'But trust me, I will.'

'One more thing,' Ashton said. 'Only we three, in this room, are to know of our marriage. When we return to Ridgeworth, we will continue as before.'

Something in Elinor's breast froze and shrank. The burst of joy that had bloomed when she first saw Ashton in that heated, sinister crush, died.

'Do not look so stricken,' Ashton said kindly. 'Our marriage may have seemed swift and almost irregular, but it will stand. And I shall own you when the time is right.'

'One of your strategies,' Dixon said, grinning.

Ashton grinned back. 'Maybe.'

It was ungrateful and illogical, Elinor

knew. She was beyond fortunate. But she did not want clever strategies or even kindness. She wanted Ashton to love her and acknowledge his love.

The journey back was uneventful and she could not fault Ashton's care. But he was just as likely to show care and concern for his horses. She sat in silent misery, unable to examine her feelings. So much had happened in such a short time. At one point she roused herself to ask, although hardly caring about the answer, 'Are we to go straight back to Ridgeworth?'

'No.' His voice was abrupt. 'I am sorry. I have a problem that concerns me. We will return to Salisbury for another night or two while I attempt to unravel the matter. Nothing that need trouble you.' He turned and smiled at her. 'Besides, you also need to acquire new clothes.'

She could not dispute that. But how difficult would that be when she could not speak of anything that had happened? 'What shall I say to the

Haddons? How am I to account for my absence?'

'Indeed. And mine also.' He frowned. 'Leave that to me. We shall say someone at the inn told you where you might find proof of your identity. I suggest the boy I used for messages, if you need to give any detail. But you can say you are weary and do not wish to speak of it.'

'Yes. And also how distressed I am because once again, it led nowhere.'

He nodded approval. 'Good. And Elinor, do not worry. When we return to Ridgeworth, we shall announce our union. It is merely that I wish one certain person to be the first to hear of it.' He paused, smiling grimly. 'The lady who is at present choosing her bride clothes in the company of my aunt.'

'Oh! Of course. I had forgotten all about her.'

'I can assure you I had not. And if you are strong enough, we will greet her together and witness her reaction.'

Elinor said slowly, 'I see.'

'You can manage this? I would not

want you to do it if not.'

'No, I am sure I can. It is just — is that not somewhat harsh?'

He said with sudden ferocity, 'She and her accomplice were harsh when they left you for dead. That was unforgivable. I intend they shall get what they deserve.' He shook his head, adding more gently, 'No, I am frightening you. Be assured, I will not be directing my anger at you. None of this is your fault.'

Elinor shook her head. 'I am not frightened, merely surprised.'

'Good. Elinor, you are safe and secure now. This may be a marriage of obligation and necessity, but I am determined you shall be content.'

As she was returned to Mrs Haddon's care, their story was almost true, she felt. She was weary beyond belief, on the verge of weeping, and the past days seemed so fantastical that she could hardly believe any of it had happened. Much less feel the need to speak of it.

Contentment seemed an unobtainable dream.

8

With the most pressing matters addressed, Ashton felt able to deal with the strange matter of Granger's whereabouts. What would have caused his agent, usually so reliable, to abruptly change his plans?

He knocked at the door of the neat and respectable house in one of the outlying villages, wondering what he might find. Granger had hardly been leaving Ashton in the lurch, as the agent had all but completed his task; but it seemed unlike him. Ashton hoped it was nothing too serious.

The little maid bobbed in confusion as she opened the door. 'Oh, sir! We were not expecting you.'

He smiled, following her in. 'No matter.'

And here was Miss Granger, sitting quietly at the fireside, mending a child's shirt. She smiled as she rose. 'What a pleasant surprise. Robert has gone to the vicarage for his lessons, all thanks to you, so I am afraid he is not here at present.' As they sat down, she added, smiling again, 'May I wish you every happiness? And is my brother with you?' Something in his face must have disconcerted her. 'I am sorry, I assumed . . . Is it too soon? Has all not gone as planned?'

'It is all going well,' Sir Ashton said easily. 'Thank you.'

'Perhaps I should not have said anything. But my brother told me something of his errand. Such a romantic story. I live very quietly here; he tries to entertain me with news when he can.'

'No, of course I do not mind your knowing.' He thought quickly. He did not want to cause her undue concern. 'And I am here again merely to check on one or two details Granger had queried. He was able to spend a fair amount of time with you while in the area here, I hope? I did suggest that he should.'

She nodded. 'Yes, and that was most kind of you. He was busy, of course, but hopeful he had achieved what you asked of him.' She leaned forward, eyes serious. 'I am glad you have come. I have hardly ever seen him so content and happy to be busy in employment he enjoys. I know he will serve you well. And thank you so much for giving him the post.'

'The least I could do. I am glad I am now in a position to be of help — and hope to do more.' He hesitated. 'The boy is well?'

'Yes, thank you.'

'And your father?' This way, his question seemed merely a polite enquiry.

Her face was shadowed. 'As far as I know. My brother hopes that he and I may be reconciled eventually, but there is no sign of that as yet.'

It was possible that their father could be ill and Miss Granger not know of it, he supposed. But if it had been serious enough for Granger to leave his post as he had, surely he would have let her know? Again, there might not have been time. And after all, Granger had done everything required of him; he would have considered Elinor to be securely escorted with Trigg the coachman and her new maid. Ashton would just have to wait until Granger returned when no doubt all would be made clear. He hoped it would not be too long. Already he had found Granger to be invaluable.

★ ★ ★

After their return to Ridgeworth, Elinor began to wonder whether she had dreamed the whole thing. There was only the ring, which she was now wearing on her right hand, to remind her. If asked, she was prepared to imply that it had been her mother's, retrieved from their house in Salisbury; but even Mrs Haddon did not remark on it. Sir Ashton did not betray by a word or a look that she was now his wife. There were the servants, of course; she supposed that given his lack of faith in their loyalty, he might fear that word could reach London and the guilty parties take flight.

But on the third day of much-needed rest, and feeling fully recovered, she was no longer in any mood to sit back and await developments. She went downstairs before Ashton could be off about the estate business which had occupied him so much and kept him out of her way. Her early rising was rewarded as she saw him going into the library. 'May I speak to you, Sir Ashton?'

He said, 'Of course. If you feel up to it. And indeed I can see that you are looking much better. I regret trailing you across two counties so soon. I could have waited.'

Did he also regret their marriage? A decision made in such haste and repented at leisure? No purpose in asking. No doubt he would only say he had made his promise and regrets were inappropriate. She said, 'Oh yes, I am fully recovered now. I wanted to ask when are you expecting the . . . other lady to return?'

'I am sorry, I should have told you. I sent a message to my aunt in London the day we came back, expressed in very general terms. I expect them tomorrow. And I hope we may confront her together, as soon as she sets foot in the house. Will you be able to cope with that?'

'Yes.' Her heart was beating faster at the thought of it but it had to be done.

'Also, the servants have found the bag your predecessor had with her when she arrived. It was hidden at the back of her wardrobe.'

Elinor frowned. 'A bag?'

He said gently, 'I have no doubt it will be yours, stolen from you after the attack. Mrs Haddon has it now. Go and look at it.'

He did not suggest that it might trigger her memories, but he must be thinking so. She hurried back to her room, quivering with excitement and fear.

Another of those times when yet again, she was almost to remember. She lifted the bag. The worn, rubbed handles felt comfortable in her hands. The bag was shabby, the leather faded and scraped, obviously belonging to someone of limited means. Her fingers were trembling as she opened it. The smell made her gasp; a scent of old leather and dust and lavender, bonding together to bring a wave of the familiar. But not enough to open the closed window within her mind. She lifted her head, dazed, almost surprised to find herself still in her new bedroom.

She looked inside. Would there be anything left? No doubt the girl's rapacious fingers had leafed through her poor possessions and rejected these few items. There were a scarf, a pair of gloves, a dried and faded posy and a small, worn testament, the pages torn and thin through much use.

She thought, *Could this have been*

my mother's? Tears choked her for a moment. She turned to the flyleaf and read the name: Amelia Wellspring. This *was* her mother's; she was certain of it. How fortunate the other girl had not taken it, to provide proof of her false identity maybe. And yet, there was something not quite right.

Mrs Haddon said quietly, 'Sir Ashton asked me to go through the young lady's room and bring everything to you that obviously belongs to you. He thought you might not care to do that yourself.'

'That was . . . thoughtful of him.' She was within a hair's breadth of allowing herself to be overcome by ready tears. She wanted to weep for the mother she had lost twice, for worst of all was her sorrow at not being able to remember her. But if once she began, she knew she would not be able to stop.

'Shall I leave you to yourself?' Mrs Haddon asked quietly.

'No, please do not. We have too much to do. I need to decide which dress to wear for the meeting tomorrow.'

'It seems a strange way of going about it,' Mrs Haddon said, 'but no doubt Sir Ashton knows what he's doing. As I see it, that girl will be arriving here, fully expecting to prepare for her nuptials, only to find that any preparations are to be for yours.'

Distracted by her emotions, Elinor opened her mouth to say there was no need for the ceremony had been performed already. And surely it would hardly matter if Mrs Haddon, who had become such a staunch and loyal friend, knew the truth? Yet she had promised and it seemed as if her life at present was twisted and bound around by promises, her own and those made by others. Deep within her being, she knew that breaking any one of them was not a choice open to her. She said only, 'Yes, I suppose so. After all the excitement she must be feeling, I could almost be sorry for her.'

★　★　★

Sir Ashton assured her they would have due warning of the arrival. He had stationed one of the farm boys on the road; while the carriage made its way along the boundary wall and the length of the drive, taking the long way round, the lad would run straight across the estate fields, crossing the river by the old wooden bridge. 'It is little enough, I know, but better than nothing. I considered arranging for someone to be at the last inn where they will have stayed, with a fast horse — but decided against it. There must be no warning. My coachman is no fool.'

'Was it he who attacked me?' Elinor tried to keep the tremor from her voice.

'Yes, I believe so, but I have no intention of your seeing him. He will be restrained as he takes the carriage to the stable yard. I will interview him myself and he will be sent to trial and imprisoned or transported. Have no doubt of that.'

Elinor shuddered. 'I am glad of it. But if I am needed to give evidence, to ensure he meets the fate he deserves, I will do it.'

'No need. You are now my wife and I will be able to speak for you.'

Elinor nodded, relieved. 'Indeed, since I cannot remember anything, I could hardly say anything useful.' She rose, saying lightly, 'I had better make myself ready.'

He nodded, his eyes appreciative. 'Only if you wish it. You look charming. That dress becomes you and you obviously have excellent taste. You will do very well as you are.'

The compliments were polite and sincere but restrained. She had a sudden ridiculous wish that he would enfold her in his arms and whisper the encouraging sentiments into her ear, before kissing her. What could she be thinking of? This would not do. Theirs was to be a marriage of obligation and convenience.

There was a knock at the door. 'Sir Ashton, your messenger is here.'

Ashton smiled at her. 'I am afraid

there is no further time to do more. If any more were needed, which it is not.' He reached out a hand and smoothed a single curl. Had it been out of place, or was this only an excuse to distract her? She was aware of the warmth of his fingers and shivered. He clasped her hand. 'Do not be afraid. They cannot hurt you now. I am here to protect you. Now and forever.'

She said, 'Thank you.' She was grateful that he had misunderstood the reason for her shiver.

'Come, we will position ourselves in the drawing room.'

She was gaining the impression he had planned everything with great care. Would there ever be a time when she would no longer be the subject of other people's plans? Even if they had her best interests at heart, as Ashton and Charles both had?

In all too short a time, the door opened and she was bobbing politely for Sir Ashton's aunt, Lady Pargeter: a smiling, talkative lady. 'Ashton my dear, what a journey. Your own coachman — and very good he is, too — was unwell, so we had to leave him behind and call upon mine. And you know how he is — tends to be grumpy at the best of times. I should pension him off, I know, but he will not hear of it. So we made a later start than intended. Oh, you have a guest — I am so sorry. How I do rattle on. Come, Elinor, I am quite hiding you away. Allow Sir Ashton to see how beautiful you are now.'

The girl obeyed, her eyes widening and the colour leaving her face.

'Ladies,' Sir Ashton said quietly, 'allow me to present my wife.'

9

Elinor curtsied again, with more deliberation this time, and the other two returned the courtesy. She said, 'It is a pleasure to meet you, Lady Pargeter.'

'And I you, of course.' Lady Pargeter's kindly face was troubled. 'Ashton, what a surprise. I hardly know where to begin. I think I must sit down.'

'I did not intend to shock you, Aunt.'

'But I am afraid you have, although I wish you every happiness, naturally.' She shook her head. 'So you have changed your mind. I have to admit, I thought it wrong of your grandfather to ever ask it of you. But what of Miss Buckler?' She gestured towards her companion, who had made no attempt to sit. 'None of this is her fault.'

'No, it is not. But the young woman beside you is not Miss Buckler. This lady, my new wife, is Miss Elinor

Buckler. Or was, before our marriage.'

Elinor felt as if she had become someone else, watching a play unfold. Perhaps Ashton had counted upon his aunt's presence making this drama easier for his new wife, as Elinor had no need to say anything. If so, she was grateful to him.

'But Elinor, or whoever you are — ' Lady Pargeter turned to the other girl. ' — what has happened? How can this be?' There was a silence as they all looked at her, waiting for her answer. For a moment, Elinor wondered whether the girl before her, dressed in the height of fashion, ringlets fetchingly arranged beneath an elaborate bonnet, would try to deny it. The colour was returning to her face as she became more calm. Even now she might try to maintain that she was Elinor, and Elinor herself an impostor.

Sir Ashton said, 'I think you will find that this is a Mary Plover, hired in Salisbury as a maid for my future wife.'

Lady Pargeter gasped. 'Oh, can this

really be true? I do not know what to think. How dreadful.'

Mary said with a sudden desperation, 'I never wanted to do it. But he made me. You only see the polite face he shows to you.' She was turned half to Ashton but more to Lady Pargeter. As yet, she had not faced Elinor at all.

'Who?' Lady Pargeter said. 'Who do you mean? Did this person threaten you?'

'The coachman. He is a distant cousin of my mother. He recommended me when Sir Ashton needed a maid to be hired for Miss Buckler. I was so pleased. I saw it as such an opportunity.' Her face was anguished; she seemed not far from tears. 'I had no idea what he intended. He'd thought it all out. When he attacked you, Miss Elinor, I was as shocked as you were. I didn't want to go along with it, after. But he said it was too late and I was involved already. He said no one would believe anything else and I must throw in my lot with him.'

Elinor frowned a little. Someone had said they would not be a party to murder. But surely that had been a man's voice? A voice that had been crisp, determined and steel-cold.

'A masterly performance,' Sir Ashton said. 'I congratulate you. I wondered how you might try and extricate yourself.'

Mary sobbed, 'He said he would kill me too.' She took a step towards Elinor, clasping her hands together. 'You must believe me, please. I thought my eyes were playing tricks on me. When I saw you here, after believing you tragically and unlawfully murdered, I thought you'd come back to haunt me. I am so glad to see you whole and unharmed and restored to your rightful place.'

'You cannot expect us to believe *that*,' Sir Ashton said.

Mary turned to Lady Pargeter. 'And I am so grateful for everything you have done for me. You have been kindness itself. And so generous and helpful when I know little of polite society. But all the time I had a cold weight on my heart, knowing what my cousin had done. I did not know how I could bear the guilt of it. I was certain at every turn and each time I opened my mouth that I would say something to betray myself and I would be found out.' She turned back to Elinor. 'I am so sorry. I fully deserve my fate. I know I must be transported at the very least. Nothing less will do to punish me.'

Sir Ashton made a contemptuous sound. 'You have the right of it there.'

Elinor did not know what to believe or suggest. She said to Sir Ashton, 'Is that really necessary, when she is so ready to repent of what she has done?'

'You mean, she makes a good representation of repentance.'

'Maybe so, but to punish someone who has been forced to act in that way?'

'And what would be your alternative? But I will not discuss this further in front of her.' He rang the bell and gave instructions to Merrill that this young woman was to be kept securely in one of the storerooms until further notice. Lady Pargeter had her lips pressed close together as if taking care to suppress her comments.

At the door Mary turned, looking from one lady to the other with a tear-stained face. 'Miss Elinor, I am so sorry, truly so. I did not want you harmed. And Lady Pargeter, I so regret having to deceive you when you have been so kind. There were so many occasions when I could hardly prevent myself telling you all of it and throwing aside my cousin's threats. Please.'

Sir Ashton said, 'Thank you, Merrill.' The door closed behind them.

Lady Pargeter, able to speak at last, said, 'Well! You never cease to amaze me, Ashton. You are full of surprises. Of course if you had told me sooner, before we set off for London, I might have revealed all and spoiled every-thing. I know I talk far too much.'

'No, no,' Sir Ashton said. 'At that time I did not know myself that Mary was anything other than she claimed to be.'

Lady Pargeter said, 'Oh, I do not mind it. I was so pleased to receive your invitation, asking for my assistance in preparing your new bride. I was finding life among the London dowagers sadly dull. But I never anticipated such a degree of excitement.'

'Neither did I,' her nephew said.

Lady Pargeter turned her attention to Elinor, reaching out to take her hands. 'And you are truly Elinor Buckler? I have to say I was surprised to find no family resemblance in — Mary, is it? I am usually considered quite skilled at that kind of thing.' She regarded Elinor kindly, her head on one side. 'Although I cannot discern a likeness in you either. Perhaps you more resemble your mother's side? But no doubt I shall discover something as we go on — a way of speaking, a turn of the head. Such things can be very telling and become obvious on closer acquaintance.'

159

'No doubt.' Sir Ashton smiled at her. 'But Elinor is now my wife, for better or worse. I am sorry the introduction was unconventional.'

'Oh, I do not mind that either. I am sure we shall be friends, shall we not, my dear?'

Elinor smiled too. 'I do hope so.'

'And you must tell me all about yourself.'

'She cannot, Aunt,' Ashton said. Briefly he explained, yet again. Elinor closed her eyes. How many times must she hear this before her memory returned? But it must come back. She was determined of that. Lady Pargeter was exclaiming in distress and sympathy. Ashton said briskly, 'So the impostor will be heard and judged fairly. I only regret that for the moment, Trigg will not be joining her there. But I intend to find him.'

'I am sure we will all welcome that,' Lady Pargeter said. 'Now, I shall go to my room and recover from the journey — and also from the excitement of the last hour.' She smiled. 'I am so pleased to meet you, my dear; and I congratulate you on your choice, Ashton.'

Again the door closed. Elinor felt her shoulders drooping as she released a deep breath of relief. 'That was not easy. I am glad it is done with. We can begin to relax a little.'

'An ordeal for you. I am sorry I had to subject you to it, but you acted with great dignity. Well done. And now, that is an end to such unpleasantness. This is the beginning of a new life for you. I must introduce you to the servants as my wife and give you a tour of your new home, in your own right.'

'I shall do my best.'

'It was strange for me too at first — being brought up to feel my true inheritance here would never be realised, and then to have it suddenly thrust upon me.' He smiled. 'We shall learn together.' He took her hands in his and bent forwards a little. Elinor closed her eyes, heart beating rapidly, certain he must be about to kiss her.

A brief knock on the door introduced Merrill once more, discreet and soft-voiced as always. Elinor strolled over to the floor-length windows and smiling, enjoying the view of the park. There would be time for many kisses.

'I shall come at once,' Ashton was saying, although his voice gave no hint of urgency. 'Excuse me, my dear. There is something I need to attend to. I shall not be long.'

She returned his smile and wandered around the room. She must accustom herself to living with such fine furnishings, although a closer look showed that Ashton's grandfather had not perhaps cared for his new home as he should. A stained rug, a drooping fringe — these were matters that could be rectified, and she would show herself willing to put things right. Being in charge of this large house was a daunting prospect; but for Ashton's sake, she would do her best.

The door opened and she turned to greet her husband with a glad smile.

His face was dark. She said hesitantly, 'Is something not well?'

Ashton did not look at her as he walked over to the window, staring out at the trees across the lawns. 'We shall see. I am not sure that everything is entirely resolved. Not as yet. There is one thing in particular that puzzles me.'

Elinor supposed there could be several. She regretted her choice of words. 'What is that?'

'This strangely convenient illness suffered by my coachman, which I do not believe for a moment. How did he know you and I were married and his plan discovered?'

Elinor stared at him, puzzled. 'Oh! But how do we know that? Perhaps he is indeed ill.'

'I very much doubt it. Heaven knows where he is now. It is highly probable that he is not even in London.'

She tried to answer his question. 'We told no one, purposely. At the inn, we behaved as if nothing had changed.'

'So how has he found out?'

'I do not know.'

Sir Ashton's voice was cool and deliberate. 'I know that I told no one. And you?'

How fortunate she had not after all confided in the motherly Mrs Haddon. That meant she could make a complete and honest denial. 'No, I know I have not.' She added, 'I was tempted to tell Mrs Haddon, who has been kindness itself to me. But I can assure you I resisted the impulse.' She met his eyes without flinching.

'So, I can only repeat it. How has he found out? Who could have known?' He was using that cool and contained voice he had directed towards Mary. He was not, as yet, angry — or not with her; but she felt that his anger was being quashed with difficulty.

She could feel her own anger rising. She was angry with both Ashton and Charles for placing her in this position when she could not defend herself. 'I did not tell anyone. You have to believe me. No one knew of our marriage.' She stopped suddenly, aware of the colour draining away from her face.

Charles. He had followed them to Salisbury and Dixon had seen him in London. Could he have found out about their hasty wedding? But why should he send a warning to the coachman? Surely he did not know him? Or did he?

Deep in thought, she had forgotten that implacable gaze. Sir Ashton said, 'You have remembered something.' It was not a question.

'Oh! No, I was trying to remember what happened in London. Whether Trigg might have caught sight of me. Of us? Or maybe we were in the wrong part of town. I do not know London at all, to say, one way or the other.' Her voice trailed to a halt.

Sir Ashton gave an angry sigh. 'I wish I could believe you. But it is not the first time I have been uncertain of your responses. I have been telling myself I have never lost my memory. That it would be unjust to assume you would

165

respond in a certain way when I have no idea of what it is like for you. However, now I cannot ignore how your face is showing me you know more than you will admit.'

Elinor stared at him in horror, saying nothing. What could she say?

He continued, 'I believed on seeing the maid's reaction I had made the right choice, as she was obviously a fraud and could not deny it. But now I am wondering whether I have merely exchanged one mistake for another.'

'Please, I do not want you to think that.'

'Of course you do not. If you are just another fortune hunter, you want me to accept you. A wealthy marriage is obviously in your best interests.'

'I am not a fortune hunter. I am sure I am not.'

'And yet you have lied to me.'

She hesitated. 'Not as such.'

'What is that supposed to mean? It seems I have done well with my choice of wife, I must say. I have been a fool.'

'No.' Her voice was filled with anguish.

He said quietly, 'I allowed my feelings to overcome my judgement. I should have followed my grandfather's way and kept to pure, cold calculation throughout the process.'

His feelings? Did that mean he could have loved her? It was like having a door opened tantalisingly, to see a golden vista filled with joy and promise on the other side. Only to have it slammed in her face. She said firmly, 'You have already told me you cannot trust the servants who were employed by Charles. What about one of them carrying tales?'

'Indeed. I should have acted on these suspicions before. Fortunately, there are not many of the original servants remaining. Several left when my grandfather arrived. And there have been more since I came here. I shall speak to the butler and the housekeeper, who were appointed by my agent and on their advice, have any others dismissed. At once.'

Elinor gave a relieved sigh. That must mean her night-time assailant would be dismissed too, surely. Without thinking, she said, 'So then we may feel safe?'

'One might hope so.' He frowned. 'I was not aware you did not feel safe. And I still consider that you are withholding something from me. No, do not try to deny it. When we were in Salisbury, I saw and recognised Charles. And so did you.'

Elinor tried to contain a gasp. She must distract him, and quickly. The night-time attack was still foremost in her thoughts. 'If we are discussing information withheld, I believe you have not told me all *you* might. What happened to your first wife?'

At once Elinor knew she had made a grave error. Ashton's face was white. He said in a low, furious voice, 'How could you have known of that? This proves me right. There is one person, more than any other, who would have told you. You did recognise Charles!'

Elinor stared at him, unable to make sense of his words. 'No! It is because of something that happened the first night I came here. Someone was in my room in the night and attacked me. And this person said I should ask you.'

'How very convenient! And why did you not think to mention this before?'

'Because at that time, I did not know who to trust.'

'So you could not even trust me — and yet you would override your doubts in order to marry me. No, I am not convinced. You can hardly be surprised. I have never heard such a weak tale.' He turned away from her, driving a clenched fist into his palm. 'Enough of all this. I do not repeat my mistakes. I have neglected this estate over the last few days and there is much to be done. When I have spoken to Merrill and Mrs Sewell, I shall spend the remainder of the day riding. I will see you for dinner. If you have decided by then whether you are willing to share your secrets with me, you may tell me so at that time.' He nodded abruptly and was gone. The door slammed behind him. She could hear him out in the hallway, calling for various servants.

She must not weep. She could hardly understand what had happened. Why had he changed towards her so completely? Something must have happened when he left the room. She wished she had tried to hear what Merrill had been telling him. Even so, if only she could feel free to tell Ashton the whole truth about Charles and her rescue, there would be no problem.

There was only one course of action to take. She must find Charles and persuade him to release her from her promise. Surely he must see that otherwise, she was of no use to him at all? How could she be an advocate for restoring his fortunes and rightful position when it was all too clear that Ashton was on the brink of dismissing her? He had money and lawyers at his command and would have no problem in annulling the hasty marriage, she was sure. It had all seemed too much like a dream. But if she could only tell him the truth, maybe it was not too late to put things right.

She must go at once while Ashton was busy with his estate, and in order to have something to tell him by the time they sat down for dinner. It was possible to get there and back on foot, she decided. It was a long way by road, but there was that path along the ridge that Charles had spoken of.

She went upstairs to change into a dress more suitable for walking and was relieved to find the bedroom empty. Mrs Haddon was the only person Elinor might entrust with the news of where she was going, but better to tell no one at all.

Almost ready, she heard hooves pounding outside and glancing out of her window, saw Sir Ashton riding furiously across the park below her, crouched over the neck of a magnificent black horse. Here was evidence that Ashton sometimes rode without due care, as Charles had said. Or maybe proof only of the extent of his anger.

She could spend no more time moping here, she thought, thrusting a plain straw bonnet onto her head. She must put this right, if she could. Her husband must not feel his kindness to her had only been repaid with lies and deception.

She could not ask anyone the way, naturally, but the path along the terrace to the west was taking her in the right direction. It seemed simple enough. The ridge where the house was set to take advantage of the views ran on to become a low hill. She was certain the slope had been visible from Charles's cottage. She walked quickly, pleased that already she was feeling a great deal stronger than when they first reached Salisbury, only a few days ago. And the distance this time was not far; little over a mile, she would guess.

It was a shame there was no time for the beauty of the view. Another day, she promised herself, she would stand and take in the distant prospect over the estate, the rolling fields beyond the gardens, bounded by woods and distant hills. If she was lucky enough to still be here to enjoy it. She increased her pace.

As the hill levelled out, she came to a stile that might mark the end of the estate, with a track beyond it. She stopped, trying to work out where to go next. Yes, this lane might be the way she and Mrs Haddon had been driven when they arrived. Mr Haddon had turned along the low wall bounding Sir Ashton's land to make his way south to the entrance gates and the driveway. And she was right, for here was the path to the cottage.

She stepped out boldly, to be brought to a halt by a familiar voice. 'If you are coming to see me, I can save you the last half mile.'

'Charles! You gave me a start. I did not see you there. But yes, I was. How fortunate.' Or was it? She must not be seen talking to Charles. Not yet. She bit her lip. How she hated all this subterfuge.

He smiled, understanding her misgivings. 'There is a convenient log here where we may sit without being observed, away from the path.'

'Thank you.' She took a breath and began abruptly, 'I had to come here. Things are not right between Sir Ashton and myself.'

'Already? And I was about to congratulate you. I thought everything was progressing as we planned.'

Elinor shook her head. 'Never exactly as we planned — although the result is the same, I suppose.' She sighed, finding herself reluctant to speak of her experiences in London. But she must. Charles must know of the dangers she had faced.

His face was expressionless as she told him. 'As you say, no real harm done. And the result is achieved.' He smiled. 'I need not have troubled with my attempt to hurry Sir Ashton into protecting you.'

'What do you mean?'

He was laughing now. 'Why, the supposed highway robbers who waylaid you on the way to Salisbury.'

Elinor stared at him. 'That was you? But Charles, I was terrified.'

'If so, you gave no sign of it. I felt almost sorry for the men when they reported back to me; they were under strict instructions to do you no harm, and yet you set about them most valiantly. I found it amusing. But enough of that. What has gone wrong?'

She said firmly, 'I don't know. But Ashton suspects I am withholding something. He thinks it has to do with Trigg not returning from London and thus evading capture. He may even disown our marriage and send me away.'

'What?' Charles leaned forward, at once becoming more alert. 'We cannot allow that. It will not serve the purpose at all. Surely you are exaggerating?'

'No. He is deeply furious with me — and gravely disillusioned.'

He looked at her thoughtfully. 'You may be right. He has an inconvenient idea of honour and always has — usually only harming himself.'

'I have come to ask you to release me from my promise.'

'What promise?'

'That I would say nothing about you or having met you and the way you rescued me. Surely, he would only be grateful to you if he knew? It might even help your case.'

Charles bent his head. He said, almost to himself, 'It hardly matters now, one way or the other.' He looked up, smiling. 'Yes, tell him if you want to.' He laughed. 'And in return, there is something you can easily do, to right the wrong done to me and my family.'

Elinor said doubtfully, 'There is?'

'I left Ridgeworth in haste, forgetting my mother's emeralds. When I discovered my mistake, naturally I asked for them at once. My request was scorned. Sir Bartholomew had no right to them and neither has Ashton. I do not feel I ask too much in wanting them back.'

She agreed at once. 'That is obviously an injustice. When the two of you are reconciled, you only need to explain to him. Ashton is reasonable and honourable; he will not wish to keep anything not rightfully his.'

'I am sure you are right. But your solution would take time.' He shook his head sadly. 'I am afraid I do not have that luxury. In my current financial state, I have regrettably incurred debts. If the jewels could be restored to me, my debts could be settled with some to spare. I could live comfortably enough and avoid a debtor's prison. But my creditors are becoming more demanding by the day.' He sighed again. 'I have been too generous to my friends, I fear.'

'I want to help you. Indeed, I must. But I do not see how I can.'

Suddenly his hand was tightly around her wrist. 'Of course you can. Find them and take them.' He paused, the cold eyes once again seeking hers. 'If I do not have them, there might be, shall we say, unpleasant consequences. For both you and your husband.'

She was frozen with fear. 'What do you mean? And you are hurting me, Charles.'

He relaxed his hold, smiling. 'I only want to help you. See, when they are restored to me, I will leave if you wish and be no further trouble to you. No further need for you to plead for the reconciliation I wanted; that does not matter compared to your future happiness.'

In the trees above her, a collared dove set up with its distinctive discordant cooing, as if it echoed the jarring discord of her feelings. She rose, brushing twigs from her skirts. 'There is something else. I asked Ashton about his first wife. That seemed to convince him more than anything I must have spoken to you.'

The expression on his face changed at once. He laughed bitterly. 'And did he tell you about her?'

'No. He was too angry to tell me.'

'Not just anger. Guilt, no doubt — and fear.' His face was bleak. 'He was married to my sister. And she died.'

Elinor felt her throat tighten in compassion. 'Oh, I am so sorry. How very sad, for both of you.'

There was a fierce, harsh note in Charles's voice. 'She was found dead in bed beside him one morning.' He paused. 'It was rumoured that he had killed her.'

10

Elinor stared at him in horror. 'That cannot be true!'

Charles shrugged. 'He never denied it. They had married without my knowledge or consent. Or his grandfather's. My sister was staying with a family I trusted and he sought her out, an impressionable and vulnerable girl. He was living only in poor lodgings in London, no fit place to take Sophia. When she died, Sir Bartholomew took charge and hushed everything up. He had useful and wealthy friends. It was easy for him.'

Elinor found her voice, although her mouth was dry. 'But what happened? How did she die?'

'There were no marks on her. My belief is that she was smothered in her pillows. The rumours spoke of an inherited illness in that branch of the

Buckler family. They walk in their sleep, often becoming violent. Or so they say.'

Elinor stared at him. 'How dreadful! What a horrible affliction. And Ashton suffers from this malady?'

Charles shrugged. 'I must presume so.'

Elinor nodded. 'A terrible burden for him to bear.' Her eyes widened. 'And now I am married to him. Am I in danger?'

Charles stared at her, as if not expecting this response. 'That was several years ago. No doubt there have been other women. It has never happened to anyone else.'

'Are you sure your dislike of Ashton and his family are not leading you to exaggerate?'

He paused. 'Take no account of me. In my grief for poor Sophia, I am not being entirely rational. I can assure you, I would never have sent you to a marriage where your life would be at risk.'

She regarded him suspiciously. 'Are

you sure? And what about my being abducted and taken to London against my will? Was that also your idea? Because that did convince Ashton of the need for haste.' She was beginning to feel angry.

'Of course not. I am surprised you can think that of me. That was a most unpleasant experience for you and I was angered that anyone would consider it. But I shall discover who was responsible, believe me. I have left instructions with several contacts who will inform me when they know anything.'

Did she believe him? She was beginning to wonder how much of what Charles said was in fact true. Why had she ever thought him a safe haven?

And whatever secrets Ashton might hide, she knew she loved her husband. She wanted above all to fulfil her marriage vows and stay with him. If he would have her. 'Thank you. And I will return the emeralds to you as soon as I may.' A small price, to have

Charles out of their lives.

Charles brightened. 'That is all I ask. And now you must go back before you are missed. You came along the ridge, in full view of the windows? I suggest you return by a different route.' He gave her brief directions. 'You will be concealed in the woodland all the way.'

Elinor nodded, hardly listening. If she was now free to tell Ashton about Charles, it did not matter. Everything was now to be out in the open. But she would gain nothing by arguing the point and would only waste time.

To her relief, he did not try to kiss her. He merely took her hand briefly. 'Good luck.'

Elinor set off, taking the second path as Charles had suggested. Soon, however, she was regretting that choice. Presumably she would emerge somewhere near the stables, at the back of the house, but already the path was twisting and turning erratically. It was a long way round to cover a short distance. And instead of enjoying her walk through the shadowed foliage, she was watching her feet for patches of mud, rabbit holes and fallen branches. She tripped on an exposed root and made her decision. It was not too late to return to the open path along the ridge where the view had been so pleasant. There she could relax with the breeze on her face and think as she walked; she must decide what she would say to Ashton.

The trees to her right thinned in the distance, with sunlight whispering through. And a faint track in the grass made by rabbits or foxes seemed promising. Taking it, she was pleased when her instincts were proved right. Once again the superb view lay before her. She took in a long breath, enjoying the freshness of the air. This was so beautiful. She did so hope she would be able to stay.

Below her and a short distance away, a movement caught her eye. Her heart leapt at the sight of Ashton, still riding too fast. She put a hand to her mouth as he came to a gate and without a pause, man and horse lifted together to sail safely over. An hour or so of hard riding had obviously not diminished his anger.

The breath died in her throat. He took a second obstacle, a hedge, also successfully, and thundered across the field beyond. She could make out his face now, grimly determined. If he continued in his present course and took the next hedge, an elegant example of topiary, he would be in the gardens and galloping across the smooth green lawns. Apparently he was too angry to care.

She stared at this next hedge, which was wider than the others. Would he think to allow for that? Something on her side, hidden from the horse and rider, caught her eye. A figure was crouching there. One of the gardeners, maybe? Why on earth was he lingering in that spot, placing himself in such danger?

Instinctively she shouted a warning,

although she knew the gardener must be too far away to hear her. He would be aware of nothing but pounding hooves. Without thinking, she ran to the slope, not knowing what she could do. She was only certain that there could be an accident and the gardener could be injured, let alone the approaching rider — and if she could do anything to help, she must.

She was still too far away. If she shouted another warning and was heard, would that only make things worse? Already it was too late. Ashton and his mount were committed to the great leap over the wide mass of green leaves. The gardener must have heard them and realised the danger, for he seemed to be staying completely still. All might yet be well. She must be careful not to get in the way herself. The thoughts passed through her mind as swiftly as fire. She veered to the right a little, hoping not to distract either of them.

No, the gardener had seen her; he

was turning his head. Even at this distance she too could feel the vibration of the hooves on the other side. Everything happened at once. She gasped in shock as a brace of doves flew up suddenly, with a loud beating of powerful wings. The horse too was in mid-flight, as the birds escaped beneath its limbs. It threw up its head, trying to change direction mid-leap, but stumbled and fell on landing. Ashton was thrown, to lie unmoving on the grass.

Elinor heard her own voice shrieking, 'No!'

The horse surged uselessly in an effort to stand and then tried again, lurching to its feet and walking slowly away. Ashton lay on his back, arms spread and eyes closed.

The breath was pounding in her chest as she ran towards the still figure, to kneel beside him. 'Ashton, can you hear me?'

There was blood on the side of his head. At least he was breathing. She must get help but did not want to leave him. She looked round for the gardener. Where was he? How fortunate he had been near at hand. But she could no longer see him. She frowned. Had he gone for help already? Without waiting to see what might be needed and how badly Ashton had been hurt? She stood up, looking around as she called out, 'Hello? Where are you? Help us. Please.'

Was that something rustling in the distant bushes? It was too marked to be caused by the faint breeze. Maybe it was birds again; strange how the doves had flown up just at that moment. But that hardly mattered. She would have to seek help herself. She hesitated. Should she move Ashton to make him more comfortable?

She called again. There might be other gardeners within hearing. No, but she could hear another horse approaching at a trot. Ashton's black horse raised its head and whickered. This rider was choosing a more sensible route and taking the gate in a measured, collected way to land in the garden beside them. 'Oh, thank goodness. Charles!' Whatever was he doing here? But that did not matter. She was merely exceedingly grateful that he was. She called, 'Sir Ashton has had an accident. We need help.'

He nodded. 'So I see. Fortunate that I was out. I was watching you to make sure you got back safely. You never can tell what dangers may lie in wait. As Sir Ashton has discovered. Is he still alive?'

'Yes but I do not know how badly injured he may be. Please can you get help? I will wait with him.'

'Of course.' Charles shrugged off his coat. 'Put that over him. I will return as soon as I may.' He paused, holding his mount in. 'And then surely Sir Ashton will see that I wish him only good.'

'I am sure he will. Just go, please.' Elinor turned back to Ashton as Charles obeyed her and was gone.

She looked down at her husband. Was his breathing any the worse? She did not think so, but he was so pale. She could yet be a widow before hardly becoming a wife. She suppressed a sob. Weeping would not help him. She must stay strong while there was the slightest hope of life and eventual recovery. She would do all she could to care for him.

As she must, because already she knew she was beginning to care for him in a different way. She had known Ashton only a matter of days, but she now knew she could grow to love him deeply. If only he could love her in return. If he survived.

She leaned over the pallid face, stroking his hair. 'I love you,' she whispered. For a moment her heart leapt with hope as she thought he had heard her. His eyes flickered but did not open. She took one cold wrist and held his hand in hers, trying to warm him a little. Would they never come?

And at last the men were here and she could help to ease him onto the makeshift stretcher and ensure he was not jolted unduly.

Once back at the house, there was Lady Pargeter to share the burden, full of strength and practical suggestions as the servants put Ashton to bed and the doctor was sent for. Elinor sat at his bedside, clasping his hand, watching the still face for the slightest sign of recovery.

A man's voice said softly, 'I can watch him. There is no need for two of us to be here.'

Surprised, as she had not heard him come in, she looked up at Dixon. It was the first time that Ashton's manservant had spoken directly to her. 'Thank you. But I need to know what the doctor decides.'

'I can tell you when he arrives.'

Yes, she was certain he would. He would always be loyal to Ashton, but what was Dixon's opinion of her? Did he know of their disagreement? She said quietly, 'Thank you, but no. And I assure you, I have Sir Ashton's best interests at heart. We must both do our utmost to ensure his recovery.'

He regarded her steadily and finally nodded.

She remembered suddenly when she had last seen him and shook her head, annoyed with herself. 'Of course. I had not realised you had returned from London. Did you discover anything?' There were enemies everywhere, it seemed. It would be as well to know who they were.

'Did you expect that I would?'

She frowned. 'I don't know. I suppose I hoped you might.'

He stepped closer, lowering his voice. 'Look, I know you don't tell Sir Ashton everything. If you want to confide in me, I may be able to help you.'

Elinor stared at him. What did he mean? Did he know about Charles? And how helpless she felt, being released at last from her dangerous promise and yet unable to share everything with Ashton? Dixon would make a good ally. She knew that Ashton listened to him and trusted him. She looked down at her hands, twisting them in her lap but knowing the decision was already made. 'Yes. Thank you. I think you may.' She took a deep breath and began her account, from her first memory of the attack on her to the need to return the emeralds.

Dixon made no comment as she spoke. As she finished, he nodded briefly. 'That explains a great deal. Now we know who our enemies are.'

'Do we? But with Trigg still at large, it is not altogether helpful. And there are still so many unanswered questions.'

'I know. But you can leave all that to me. As you said, you and I need only work to ensure Ashton's recovery. And I would suggest that no one, not even you or I, is on watch alone with him. Two people at all times. If the rule applies to us also, it will not arouse suspicion.'

She glanced uneasily over her shoulder. 'So you think there are still enemies within the house?'

'We dare not assume there are not.'

Their discussion was cut short by

Merrill with the doctor and Lady Pargeter. The doctor's verdict was only what might have been expected. Rest was needed; a better idea might be had when Sir Ashton recovered consciousness. But he was young, healthy and strong.

'And a large fee for what we could have told him ourselves,' Lady Pargeter said in exasperation. 'But it is much as I thought.'

'We must just wait and hope.' Elinor trusted she sounded more courageous than she felt.

'Indeed we must. And shall, my dear,' Lady Pargeter said gently. 'I know my nephew will have the best of care. I have to admit, I was shocked and surprised this morning by Ashton's revelation — but now I am more than satisfied with the choice he has made.'

Elinor said only, 'Thank you.' If only Ashton would be happy with it.

'But there is something I must ask you.'

Did Lady Pargeter wish her to

provide further proof of her identity? Elinor was happy enough to share everything she and Sir Ashton had discovered and indeed to tell her everything she could recall of her situation. But she was unprepared for the enquiry to come.

Lady Pargeter asked quietly, 'Was that Charles Buckler who rode to the house to raise the alarm?'

Keeping her face calm took a supreme effort. 'Yes, it was.'

'Does this mean the rift between them is healed? If so, I am very surprised. And not altogether sure I consider it the wisest course.'

Elinor stared at her. Of course, Ashton's aunt must know of the family rift. Lady Pargeter's face was troubled. She rose, turning away from Elinor as she walked across the room and back again as if deliberating with herself.

Elinor said, 'I do not think we should talk about this, whatever Charles has done — or is said to have done. I feel I should hear it only from Ashton, if he thinks himself wronged.'

'I agree, my dear. But Ashton is not able to speak for himself.'

'Then we must wait until he is,' Elinor said firmly.

'You do not understand. Charles is — well, I do not think he can be trusted. Please tell me, how do you know him? I was astounded when he appeared. He did not wait to speak to me; I only glimpsed him seeking help from the servants. But clearly he knew who you were. And how did he happen to be there? I am sorry, my dear; I appear to be interrogating you. But one never knows what Charles may take it into his head to do, what new mischief.'

'But Lady Pargeter,' Elinor said, distressed, 'you are quite wrong. I have found him good and kind and without his timely appearance, I would have died.'

'Whatever do you mean?'

Again she related the whole, but this time ending with Ashton's distrust, as he came to realise she had been hiding something. However, she had no doubts about the kindness Charles had shown and could convey that as strongly as possible.

Lady Pargeter frowned. 'But how long were you staying in this cottage, in such a weak and vulnerable state — and alone?'

'No more than a week or so, I believe. And I was never alone with Charles, for Mrs Haddon was there at all times — as housekeeper, nurse and chaperone. Although I was too ill to worry about such things.'

Lady Pargeter nodded. 'I expect it will do. Besides, you are married now.'

Elinor tilted her chin, straightening her back. 'My reputation was the least of my concerns, I can assure you. I was alone and fearful. I could not remember anything. I did not even know who I was until Charles told me.'

'Yes, I suppose we must be grateful for that. And meanwhile Mary had continued the journey driven by her wicked cousin and was proceeding to convince poor Ashton she was the subject of his obligation.' She sighed. 'And she was wonderfully convincing. She must have learned a great deal about you during the journey.'

'No doubt I was only too pleased to have a sympathetic audience. I was in a new and strange situation and probably in need of someone to talk to. And all the time, she was merely thinking of what was planned. But Lady Pargeter, I am so fortunate that Charles came to my rescue. I am in his debt. I promised I would help him regain Ashton's favour and I must keep that promise. But as I told you, when Ashton rode off in anger, I took the opportunity to see Charles and obtained his permission to tell Ashton everything. Which surely will only help to wipe out whatever misdeeds are in his past?'

'I beg you to think very carefully about this.' Lady Pargeter seemed distressed. 'Speaking out blindly, without knowing what Charles has done, could be dangerous.'

Elinor nodded slowly. 'Yes, you are right. I have to know. Ashton's accident has changed everything. You must tell me, Lady Pargeter. Please.'

Lady Pargeter nodded. 'Very well. When Ashton's parents died, his grandfather could hardly be troubled with him, until it occurred to him that he could make use of Ashton in the long-standing family feud. They have all been at bitter odds for years over the inheritance of Ridgeworth. Sir Bartholomew sent Ashton to the school Charles attended, hoping to make mischief wherever he could. But the malice came from Charles.'

'From Charles?' She was already doubtful as to whether Charles always told the truth, but could hardly believe that he would be malicious.

Lady Pargeter was saying, 'There was an unfortunate circumstance concerning the headmaster's daughter — a very respectable girl I believe, and foolishly discreet. Nothing would induce her to reveal the father of her child.'

'A child?' Elinor bit her lip.

'I am afraid so. However, the information came out somehow. Gossip and rumour at the school had it that Ashton was the father.'

'Ashton?' Again, Elinor could not conceal her surprise.

'He was not, of course. But the headmaster believed the rumours and Ashton was taken away and sent to another school. His grandfather, always unpredictable, found the incident amusing. He said he had always considered Ashton a dull dog and was glad to be proved wrong.'

'Did the truth never come out?'

'Ashton refused to deny it.'

'And that poor girl?'

Lady Pargeter shook her head. 'I do not know. But the likelihood is that Charles was the father.'

Rumour and likelihood? Elinor was not convinced, but clearly Ashton had acted honourably. She said slowly, 'We were terribly at odds before the accident. Over Charles. And now, how can I tell him? Even when he wakes, the shock of hearing how I have deceived him could cause a relapse.' She put her hands over her face.

'Ashton knows Charles only too well. He will not blame you for being taken in, as many others have been. Only, be sure to leave nothing out, and Ashton will understand.'

'Thank you, Lady Pargeter,' Elinor said, standing up. 'You have been very frank. And now, I have been away from Ashton for too long. I must see how he is.'

Lady Pargeter put out a hand as if to prevent her. 'My dear, do take care. You are barely recovered yourself and you need rest. And after such a day as you have just had — and such a week. The servants will call you if there is any change.'

Elinor hesitated. 'Ashton does not entirely trust all of them. Those who were employed by his grandfather, in particular.'

'So we will be careful. And you can

trust his man, Dixon — that I can tell you. They met in London years ago; he would give his life for Ashton. I believe Ashton was instrumental in saving his.'

It was good to hear that Lady Pargeter's judgement echoed hers. 'I have already spoken to him. No one will be left alone with my husband; the servants will keep watch in pairs, and only then if Dixon or I have approved them.'

'An excellent idea. And I will be more than happy to sit with him myself. My maid can be my companion.'

Elinor accepted the offer gratefully. It seemed strange, but although everyone kept telling her how tired she must be, she still felt alert and on edge. All she needed was time to sit quietly and try to think. And she could do that while attending on Ashton.

Lady Pargeter left to help organise the sickroom watches as Dixon returned. 'How is he?' he asked.

Elinor rested her hand on his forehead. 'He does not seem unduly hot. A little restless after the doctor's visit, but peaceful again now.' She wished she could say the same of herself. Her thoughts were in confusion. Everything had seemed clear, but now she did not know what to believe. Charles had seemed so kind — but for Charles, would a week of seeming kindness be a small price to pay, when the possible reward would be so great?

She knew at last what he wanted: the return of the misplaced jewellery. And she could understand that. Once he had the emeralds, they need never see him again. That would be the best possible outcome.

Dixon said softly, 'We must not disturb him. I suggest we speak in low voices and move over to the window.'

She agreed, following with a backward look towards the pillows. And it seemed that Dixon had been reading her thoughts and wanted to help her. He murmured, 'Perhaps it would be best if you could return the emeralds as quickly as possible.'

'Oh, yes. I want nothing more than to be rid of Charles. But I do not know where they are.' She glanced around the room.

He smiled. 'I do. In the top left-hand drawer of the mahogany tallboy in the dressing room. You will need this key. I will watch over Ashton here while you slip in.' And as she hesitated, 'We will be in your view at all times if you leave the door open, see. It will be as if you'd never left the room.'

11

Glancing towards the sleeping Ashton, Elinor tried the key in the left-hand drawer in the tallboy, feeling uncomfortably like a thief. This was ridiculous; Ashton had offered the jewels to her on their first evening here. And how long ago that seemed.

She held her breath. This was necessary if Charles were to be dealt with. But she would not want Ashton to learn of it too soon. And not merely by watching her. Better maybe if she had closed the door. When the drawer opened almost silently, she breathed out with relief.

Behind her, Ashton shifted and moaned slightly. She slid the drawer shut and moved quietly to stand beside Dixon, heart thudding. Ashton's eyelids flickered. Dixon shook his head. She ignored him as she said quietly,

'Ashton? Can you hear me?'

There was every possibility that he could. She could remember, after her accident, being more aware than Charles and Mrs Haddon had realised. To her disappointment, however, Ashton did not respond, and now he was lying quietly once more.

She sighed and returned to the two small drawers, again sliding the first open with no sound. Yes! These must surely be jewellery boxes. There were two. She wanted to snatch at them but made herself examine each carefully. The larger held a confusion of all kinds of adornments, mostly with old-fashioned settings, some with stones missing, although no doubt they were of value if they could be sorted and repaired. A second, smaller box held only a diamond necklace. This was taking too long. Was she following Dixon's instructions correctly?

Yes — at last, here it was: the slim casket she recognised. Green fire was briefly revealed in a gleam of sunlight from the tall window. She closed the lid to conceal them again, her heart beating.

She did not need to take the box. Only Dixon would know the contents were missing. That would give her the time she needed to deliver the emeralds to Charles, to choose the right moment to tell Ashton what she had done and how she had acted for their joint benefit. If Ashton should ask for them, she knew now she could trust Dixon to explain if necessary.

It seemed like ages, but it must have taken only moments, to remove the emeralds, hide them in her pocket and replace the box in the locked drawer, and then to return the key to Dixon, who was smiling encouragement. Even so, her fingers were sliding clumsily in her haste. At any moment, Ashton might wake.

But no. It was done. She sat down by the bed with sweat breaking out on her forehead. And now, whole-heartedly, she did wish Ashton would wake. It was also a relief just to sit and recover her strength, although she had managed all of this surprisingly well. She had to feel satisfied about that.

It was to be her last waking thought before opening her eyes with a start to the room now dim in the dusk. For all her satisfaction at her recovery, she had slept as she sat there. She said, 'Ashton?'

Dixon appeared at her side. 'Nothing has changed.'

'You should have woken me.' But Dixon was right. Ashton was lying there, pale and still, and there was no knowing how he would react to his new wife when he did wake.

At least in all the turmoil of what had to be done, she had made a beginning. She studied his face; the strong lines were now relaxed, reminding her of the qualities she so liked in him: the determination, the kindness, the flashes of humour. He must recover. She could not bear it if he did not. She leaned forward, suddenly alert. Was his breathing a little easier? She placed her hand on his brow again. Surely he was cooler?

He opened his eyes.

Her own eyes widened in shock. She gasped and held her breath, not wanting to startle him.

He said, 'Elinor?'

'You know me?' She fought back the tears. 'Thank goodness. I thought you might have forgotten. As I did.'

'Ah. Because of the blow to the head. No.' He smiled. 'Whatever happens, I will never forget you.'

Whatever happens. In spite of his smile, the words had an ominous sound and her heart sank. She said gently, 'What must happen now is that you must recover completely.'

He frowned. 'There were birds — doves or pigeons I think — flying out under Thunderer's hooves.'

'Hush. You are not to worry about anything.'

His voice was drowsy now. 'So I will not. If that is what you tell me.' He closed his eyes and by the calm of his breathing, she could tell he was sleeping easily.

She murmured, 'Rest and time. That is what is needed.' And love. She did not think she had said it aloud. She sank back into her chair, only now realising how exhausted she felt. The worst of her anxieties were over; he was on the way to recovery and remembered her. Dixon said quietly, 'You need to rest. It seems as if the worst is over.'

'No. I will stay awake now.' But when she opened her eyes once more, Ashton was watching her, half-smiling.

She struggled out of a deep sleep. 'Oh, no! How could I do that again? I am supposed to be watching you. How long have I slept?'

Lady Pargeter's voice said, 'You needed the sleep, my dear. I fully agreed with Dixon when I came to relieve him. And how that man manages on so little sleep is beyond my understanding. It is fully dark now and he will be here again in a moment.'

Ashton said, 'And now I am telling you that I am well guarded with all your arrangements and you must go to bed. You are hardly recovered yourself.'

'I will go when Dixon comes,' she said firmly. 'You will be safe with him.'

'Good. He can stay for the rest of the night.'

'Yes. That is what we have arranged.'

'You seem remarkably organised. Ah, here he is now.'

She smiled at Dixon, who was unable to prevent the pleasure showing on his usually stern face. She said, 'Sir Ashton has come round. But he is still tired and needs to sleep if he can. At least to rest.'

Dixon nodded. 'I'll see to it, my lady.'

She said quietly as she passed him, 'Please do not let him ask questions about pigeons and how the accident happened.'

'I can manage him.'

'I am not here to be managed,' Ashton said irritably. 'You cannot hide things from me. I shall find out what I need to know.'

'Yes, of course. But not now,' Elinor said. She and Dixon exchanged a smile. From now on, the two of them could work together in Ashton's mutual interest. She walked along the landing, knowing a great weight had been lifted from her heart, but there was still much to do. She must sleep now to be awake early, as she had one more urgent task to perform. It was of the utmost importance to pass the emeralds over to Charles, seeing him safely on his way before Ashton was fully recovered.

She slept but not deeply, knowing even while sleeping how she must set out and return before she was missed. She had decided to take Mrs Haddon into her confidence about the timing and direction of her errand but not its full purpose. As it happened, the first lightening at her windows woke her without any assistance. Mrs Haddon was only moments behind her. 'Shall I come with you?'

'Thank you, no. I need you here in case Sir Ashton should ask for me. You can say I am still asleep. Dixon will support you.'

'At least take Mr Haddon. I can wake him in moments; he is only in the stables.'

'Two people are more noticeable than one. I will be better alone. I will go through the woods; it is a little further, but much less visible.' She had taken care to discover where the path Charles had suggested emerged, near the house. And she had only told Mrs Haddon she had some final business with Charles. She had said nothing about the emeralds.

Elinor hoped she would not meet any of the servants as she left, aware that they began work early. She was ready to say she needed fresh air after her long hours in the sick room. Not that it should be their place to question her actions; she was now entitled to go wherever she chose. This was still something she needed to become accustomed to. However, when she had discovered this entrance the other day, no one had noticed her. She assumed this corridor was little used.

As she slipped into the narrow passageway, someone was coming in from the courtyard. It was not easy to see him in the dim light; she assumed it must be one of the male servants. Forgetting her story, she instinctively dodged back out of sight, and at once berated herself. Unless she retraced her steps to the entrance hall, he would see her anyway and time would be wasted.

No, she must pass him confidently, with a greeting maybe. She paused, wondering where he was. He should be here by now. Purposefully but quietly moving forward, she saw the shadowed figure as soon as she turned the corner. He had stopped at a barred door halfway along the passageway, glancing behind him to the courtyard as he tried the bolt.

She coughed and without looking round, he turned and hurried away to the open air. Perhaps he had been trying to steal something from one of the storerooms? There were still untrustworthy servants here, it seemed. Or he could have been one of those who had left, returning for what he could find. She must see to it that the small outer door was kept locked, at least overnight.

Elinor hurried along the path, all too aware of the value of what she carried. She kept a hand on her pocket constantly, feeling the hardness of the stones, the intricate curves of the gold settings. She was making herself more nervous with every step, starting at shadows. For how would Charles react if she should lose them in some way? How would she ever be able to compensate him?

But all was well and she arrived safely, although flushed and out of breath. This time, in spite of the early hour, Charles did not seem surprised to see her. 'As a moth to a flame,' he murmured, smiling. Or that was what she thought he had said. She must have misheard him.

'I beg your pardon?'

'No matter.' He smiled. 'So how is your husband? Not in good health, I hear. Most regrettable.'

She smiled too. 'A great deal better, thank you. I have every hope he is on the way to recovery. And most fortunately his accident was in no way as disabling as mine.'

'I see. So you thought to bring me this good news in person?'

'That is not why I came. I made you a promise. We had an agreement. I have come to fulfil it.'

'Really? And what was that? Pray remind me.'

'I suppose you did not think I would accomplish my task so soon.' She brought out the emeralds, trying to handle them carefully, but they slid from her grasp to shower across the small polished table in a light-catching spray of green flame.

'Ah,' Charles breathed. 'You have succeeded indeed.'

'Here is your inheritance. Now you

can be satisfied you have received the justice denied to your family.'

'Yes.' He ran his fingers through them, holding them up to the light. 'This is very well. Very well indeed.'

'I believe so. And now I have returned them to you as I promised, I have also come to make my farewell.'

Charles stared at her. 'Your farewell? What can you mean?'

Why did she need to explain it? 'You and your family have been unjustly treated, I understand that. So it was only fair that the emeralds should be returned to you. Now you will be able to leave here and make a new start in life.'

'A new start?'

'Yes. You could ... I don't know, purchase a commission in the army perhaps. That would be a glorious life with Napoleon secured upon Elba. Or the money might enable you to be based in London among your literary equals and pursue your poetic ambitions. When your debts are paid.'

'Elinor, my dear, you have misunderstood me completely.' He laughed. 'This is just the beginning.' Before she could move, he was across the room and seizing her in his arms.

Horrified, she tried to push him away, pressing her hands against his chest. 'Charles, no. I am Ashton's wife.'

Now his laughter was harsher. 'Wife? Maybe, for now. And I doubt he appreciates you as you deserve. Has he even kissed you? What a fool he is. Let us rectify that, at least.' Before she could prevent him, his lips were upon hers.

With an effort she freed one hand and pushed it under his chin, wresting her face away. 'No. How dare you?' They stared at each other. There was fury in his eyes but she must not show fear.

He looked away first, passing the moment off with a shrug. 'I am sorry. But can you blame me, faced with a young woman of such beauty?'

'You could have asked me to marry

you in the first place, when I was so afraid of the outside world and would have welcomed your protection.' She knew as she spoke that this would not have been a sensible basis for marriage.

'Impossible, my dear. As I explained, I could not have supported you appropriately.'

'No. And you cannot change your mind now.'

'We are all at the mercy of our mistakes. I can only apologise. I had forgotten what an honourable creature you are. And of course while your marriage lasts, we must be circum-spect.'

She said firmly, and more confidently than she felt, 'It will last. I can put everything right.'

He shrugged. 'It is as I told you from the start. The result of Ashton's reckless riding is all too clear. How many times could he repeat that and survive? He has been fortunate this time.'

She closed her eyes, hardly listening. Ashton had every cause for his recklessness that morning. It was all her fault. 'Everything will be all right if only we can be left to ourselves. You have what you wanted and now you must leave us alone. You promised.'

'Did I? Maybe you are right. And a promise must always be honoured. We both know that, do we not?' He moved towards her and took her hand. She shrank away but he was only carrying her fingers to his lips with a mocking look. 'Go home by all means and care for Sir Ashton. Demonstrate just how caring a wife you can be. Earn his gratitude.'

'And you are to leave this house? And go somewhere far away from here?'

'Do not worry. I will no longer be a concern for you.' He smiled. 'And with that, I am afraid, you will have to be satisfied.'

12

Satisfaction was far from what Elinor was feeling as she hurried back. Would Charles go? But he must. She was thinking as she walked of several questionable remarks he had made. She shuddered. There had been further glimpses of the other, darker Charles. More than once, before he had been swift to conceal it, there had been something sinister in his face.

She was returning by the quickest way, forgetting any need to hide herself. Already she had reached the point where she had witnessed Ashton's accident. What was it Charles had said? Ashton had approached the hedge at speed, certainly, but rashly? Ashton could not have expected the collared doves to fly up. That gardener must have disturbed them.

She stopped suddenly, breathing

hard. How stupid she had been. That man had not just disturbed them; he had released them. He was no gardener. No wonder there had been no further sign of him.

So who was he? She did not have to think too hard to come up with at least one possibility. Where now was Josiah Trigg, the coachman who had attacked her, hoping to kill her? The man who had mysteriously absconded before Mary and Lady Pargeter could be driven back from London, obviously fearing arrest or reprisal. He would be first to wish Ashton harm.

And what of Charles? She shuddered with unease. The strange remarks he had made began to make a sinister kind of sense. All those hints about what a reckless driver and rider Ashton had always been, when she had seen hardly any evidence of this. Only on that one occasion when she had known him to be hurt and angry. And as she now believed, the accident had been none of his doing. Why had Charles said such things, and repeatedly? Unless he had been preparing her for an accident he had known would happen.

Her heart was gripped with an icy horror. That would mean Charles had planned it — or had agreed to it. But why? What would that achieve? Ashton might have broken his neck, which no doubt would have pleased Charles. But even a severe fall might not lead to Ashton's death. Presumably that would be what Charles had intended.

No, Ashton could easily have died, left unconscious on the ground like that. If she had not seen him fall; if she had not ignored Charles's suggestion of taking the woodland path. Charles, yet again.

Ideas were coming thick and fast. That man she had seen. If she had not called out and gone running down the hill, what might he have done next? She shivered. All too easy for him to ensure that any harm begun by the fall could be finished off with the use of a stout cudgel. Everyone would have assumed any injuries had been caused by the accident.

She thought, *I am speculating. I do not know any of this*. But her mind would not be still. Charles's constant insistence that once she was married, she would be in a better position to help him. Had he meant, not when she was married, but when she was widowed? And a rich widow. No wonder he had seemed so kind and caring. No wonder he had kissed her.

She moaned aloud. And she had thought Charles would be satisfied with a set of emeralds — however valuable — when all along he was expecting to have everything. How stupid she had been. Believing the best of someone so deceitful when all the time, the evidence to the contrary had been staring her in the face.

At least there was no need to worry about being set upon by the would-be killer, she thought bitterly. She was essential to their plan. It was Ashton who was in danger. She must hurry back and tell him so. They must be even more vigilant, hiring in more men if necessary. If only she could persuade Ashton to listen to her.

It was still early. With any good fortune, no one would have noticed her absence. Again, no one was about in the outer courtyard, but all the same she stepped out boldly as if she had every right to be there.

Sighing with relief, she regained her room. 'I have not been missed, have I?'

Mrs Haddon seemed flustered. 'Sir Ashton sent to ask for you, not half an hour gone. I said you were not yet awake. I don't know if Dixon believed me.'

Elinor nodded. She would change into her indoor slippers, but this everyday dress was more than suitable for attending a sickroom. Once again, she hurried along the landing and fixed a smile upon her face. 'I am so sorry. Mrs Haddon should have woken me earlier. How are you this morning?' She stopped. She was speaking to an empty bed. She looked around the room and Sir Ashton was dressed and seated in a chair by the window. He was white-faced and regarding her silently. She said, 'You are up! Is this wise?'

'Where are the emeralds?'

For a moment she had no breath to reply. At last she said helplessly, 'It is too soon. You should not be troubling yourself. Where is Dixon?'

'My loyal servant has been on duty by my side all night. I have sent him for some much-needed rest. But I have only this morning discovered the emeralds are missing and so I am bound to feel troubled, as you put it. They should have been yours. Touched by your care and concern for me, I intended to give them to you, as my wife. As you must know. Indeed, when you first wore them and you refused my offer, I was impressed by your lack of avarice and sense of fitness. Now I can see how that was an act to earn my respect.'

Elinor said miserably, 'It was not an act.'

'So please, tell me why you saw fit to take them. And where you have been. Do not think to try and deny it. I saw you. I thought myself still affected by my blow to the head until I checked the box.'

'But you were still unconscious.'

'No. You only thought so.'

'I have made a terrible mistake.'

'Naturally. You have been found out.'

'That is not what I meant.' She stopped, trying to find the strength to tell him. 'I lied to you. Or at least, I did not tell you the full truth.'

'I know that. So, what exactly is this truth you have withheld? I would welcome your version. You had better sit. Here, opposite me, with your face in the light, if you please.'

Elinor took a deep breath, hoping for courage. 'It was not Haddon who rescued me when I was left for dead. It was your grandfather's predecessor here, Charles.' She stopped. Ashton's face was white and hard-set. He said nothing, neither to encourage nor condemn, his expression unchanging. 'Charles took me to shelter in the cottage he was leasing, just away from the end of your estate, in the woods there. Then his housekeeper, Mrs Haddon, nursed me back to health. They were both so kind. Charles seemed so caring and anxious for my welfare.'

'Charles. I see. And you came round unable to remember anything? Who you were or where you had been going?'

'Yes. As you know.'

'Well, it is what you have told me. If that was the case, how did you know you were on your way here? And that Mary had taken your place?'

Elinor stared at him. 'Oh. I never thought about that.' She looked down at her lap. 'Charles told me.'

'And how did he know?'

She whispered, 'I do not know.'

'Come, Elinor. You must surely have worked it out by now.'

She looked up, meeting the implacable chill of his stare. 'Charles must have known who I was all along. He must have been in league with Josiah Trigg. At first, at least.' She paused. 'But I did not know that, I promise you.'

'If I can believe a word you say.'

She said suddenly, 'It was Charles I heard! That voice, saying he would not be a party to murder. But it did not sound like Charles.' Considering this in the light of her new realisation, perhaps it had. In the cottage, he had been at such pains to speak slowly and pleasantly. Ignoring her instincts, she had made the mistake of thinking a gentle manner demonstrated gentleness of character.

Ashton said, 'Charles could always play to an audience to make the impression he wanted. I admit I can hardly blame you for being deceived. You were in a most vulnerable and difficult position. People of far greater strength and awareness than yourself, at that time, might have been readily taken in.'

'I should have realised.'

He shrugged. 'Maybe not. Even so, why did you not tell me of the true identity of your rescuer?'

'He asked me not to. I promised I would not.'

'Yes, Charles was always skilful at imposing his will. I can accept that. Even if it meant you had to lie to me. What reason did he give for exacting this promise?' Was he perhaps softening towards her? The way he sat so straight and still in his chair, arms folded, did not give that impression.

She said, 'He said there was a long-standing enmity between you. If I even mentioned his name, you would turn against the truth of my story and never believe me.'

'And my supposed reason for this long-held grudge? Did he explain that?'

'Not fully. He hinted a little. But Lady Pargeter told me of what happened when you were at school together.'

He nodded. 'Did she also tell you my grandfather regained Ridgeworth from Charles at cards?'

'Cards?' Elinor could not disguise her shock. How could Charles have been so reckless? This explained a great deal. But he had been punished severely for that moment of weakness.

Ashton was saying, 'An irregular circumstance; but as it led to the only right conclusion, I can never regret it. At the gaming tables, fortunes change hands overnight.'

'I suppose they must.' Yes, she could imagine the men she had encountered at Drury Lane being capable of such things. 'I am sorry. I know I have been very mistaken, but steering my way through this maze has been impossible.'

'True. But before we are brought to tears of regret at the sadness of your plight, you have not answered my initial question. The emeralds?'

Elinor shuddered. He was not softening towards her at all. He had been awaiting this answer all the time. In spite of her resolve, she was at a loss as to how she was to explain her actions.

He said, 'Unfortunately I believe your silence has answered me. I think I may infer the answer from what you have already said.'

'I regret it very much indeed. I am sorry. I gave the emeralds to Charles.'

He nodded. 'As I expected. You sound so plausible in your regret too.'

She said painfully, 'He said they had been his mother's and he had inadvertently left them behind when he left in haste. I believed him. I promised I would restore them to him.'

'Yet another promise. No doubt we are both far too free with our promises. And you still believe him?'

'No. Beyond any shadow of doubt, I do not. I thought if I fulfilled my promise, Charles would be content to go away and leave us alone. You and I. That was all I wanted. I took them to him this morning. I have only just returned.'

'And now you are about to tell me

your eyes are opened and you wish you had not done so.'

'That is exactly what I am saying.'

'So what has changed your mind?'

'Charles. For the first time I saw the person Lady Pargeter had described. He will not leave us, not on any account. He thinks — ' She hesitated. 'He thinks the emeralds will be just the beginning of what he is to receive.'

'He must be very sure of himself. Why would he think that?'

'He believes, if you should die, he will be able to marry me and inherit everything.'

'So, again, why would he think that?' Ashton's face remained expressionless. 'Has he received a measure of encouragement?'

If she lied, everything would be lost. With the truth, she risked losing him anyway. She tried to keep her voice steady. 'Before I ever met you, yes he had. I was completely alone. He seemed the only possible safe refuge for me. But he explained how he could not support a wife. He said I must come to you and fulfil my purpose — and see how best I might be of help to him after we were married. He did not say how I might help him; he never mentioned the emeralds, not then. It was all kept very vague.'

'It would be. And when did he mention my death would be a convenient part of this plan?'

'He has not. Not directly. I only realised the full extent of the plot when I was returning from the cottage this morning. I remembered how I had witnessed your accident. Although I am sure now it was no accident. It was deliberate. The birds were released at exactly the right moment to cause the most harm. And I firmly believe had I not been there, he would have finished the work begun by the fall.'

'I do not follow you.' His eyes were alert. 'Who would?'

'The man I saw on my side of the hedge. It could even have been Trigg, I suppose, but at that distance I could not be certain who it was. I saw everything from the path on the top of the ridge.'

'Trigg, you say? Not Charles, then? You surprise me.'

'No, I know it was not Charles. This person was shorter, more heavily built. Ashton, you have to believe me, please. I have been too easily misled, I admit that. But I met Charles before I met you. I believe — ' She stopped. But what had she got to lose? 'I know now I am beginning to love you.'

Ashton stared at her, not even blinking.

'Please say something.'

'I hardly know what to say.' At last he shifted in his chair, looking away from her to where the early sunlight was at last gilding the gardens outside. 'I hardly know what to believe. I will have to give this more thought.' He paused. 'We could have the marriage annulled.'

'Not that. Please, Ashton.'

He said quietly, 'At least then my life would no longer be in danger from

Charles and his plan would be foiled.'

She nodded, near to tears. He was right, of course. She had to admit that. And if it would keep him safe, that was what they would do. But it would break her heart. 'I understand.'

★   ★   ★

Ashton slumped back into his chair as Elinor left the room. His head was aching but that hardly mattered. He had never imagined he would lose his heart to this marriage of convenience and obligation. Neither could he have pictured anything more unwelcome. How his grandfather would be laughing if he could see Ashton now, with all the old man's mischief-making coming home to roost as planned — and more. That thought knocked him out of his despondency. There was too much to do. He would not give in to self-indulgence.

First he would question Mary again. He had been too swift to dispose of her when she might yet hold useful information. Granger, for instance. What was the real truth behind the message Mary had brought, saying Granger had discovered urgent family business he must attend to? That had seemed strange even then; he should not have accepted it so easily.

Dixon, as always, was coming into the room without needing a summons. Ashton smiled. 'Good. If Mary Plover has not yet been taken to the care of the constables, I wish to speak to her.'

He frowned as Dixon left, planning what he would ask her and how he might phrase his questions in the best way to catch her out. He knew she was clever, but not clever enough, he was certain of that. He was convinced she knew more than she had admitted.

'Sir Ashton?' Dixon's face was expressionless. 'She is not there. Some-one has opened the door and helped her to escape. I checked with Mr Merill; he was waiting for instruction from you before taking her into custody.'

Ashton swore. 'My own fault. I should have made sure she was kept more securely. Set a guard on the door, even.' Too late now. Thinking quickly, he said, 'Obviously we did not succeed in being rid of all of those loyal to Charles. Or even every last one of Trigg's relatives.'

Were both groups, those of Charles and Trigg, one and the same? Or were they now working apart and with different motives? One group must be supporting Mary Plover's deception, and Charles supporting Elinor's. If they had been all one at the start, he did not believe they were now. No wonder he had not been able to disentangle the various threads and act accordingly.

That must be why Charles had not wanted Elinor killed, as she had described — because he considered she was more valuable to him alive. Maybe he had gone along with Trigg's plan; might even have instigated it, as far as he felt it useful. Maybe he had always intended to drop and betray Trigg and his young female relative, in favour of a plan where Charles alone would benefit. A complex plan and a huge risk. But Charles had always been a risk-taker and an opportunist.

Charles could not have expected Elinor to lose her memory, but had been swift to make use of that. And even if the plan had not succeeded at all, he would take pleasure in causing Sir Ashton a great deal of embarrassment and inconvenience. In this he had been successful. He doubted whether Charles had expected himself to fall in love with Elinor, but how maliciously delighted he would be if he knew.

Ashton smiled grimly. Charles, he resolved, would regret this. Most of all, he would come to rue trying to use an innocent and vulnerable girl as a helpless pawn.

13

Elinor had walked away with her emotions half-choking her, unable to think of anything to say in her defence. How could she? All Ashton's accusations were true. She had acted rashly, giving her trust unthinkingly. Half-blinded by tears, she could hardly see where she was going.

Mrs Haddon was busy tidying the room and exclaimed at once at the sight of her. It was too late to try and conceal her feelings. 'Oh, Miss Elinor — Lady Buckler — whatever is the matter?'

'He will not forgive me for concealing my knowledge of Mr Charles. But I had promised. What else could I do?' And yet, more than once during their exchange, Ashton had seemed willing to be reasonable before again becoming cold and implacable.

'A harsh verdict indeed.' Mrs Haddon

sat down beside her, taking her in her arms, more in the nature of a mother than a servant; but Elinor welcomed the human contact. 'He is not going to cast you off, is he? Not without some kind of settlement?'

'I do not know. He is thinking about it.'

'It makes my blood boil,' Mrs Haddon said, 'to see you so badly treated and so upset. A pity he did not die in the fall if you ask me.'

'No. Never say that. I . . . love him. He is my husband. He acted honourably towards me. I would never wish him ill. All I want is to be reconciled.'

'Of course, of course. I spoke out of turn. See, you are worn out with worry and grief. Why not go back to bed, since you rose so early? I will bring a hot tisane and a warming pan.'

Meekly, Elinor allowed herself to be persuaded. Rest would be beneficial; she must recover her strength in order to plead her case when the time came.

True sleep was not possible; she

dozed fitfully while trying to gather her thoughts. Lady Pargeter would surely be an ally also. But what would she feel about the loss of the emeralds? And perhaps Dixon had not yet had the opportunity to speak for her.

One moment her thoughts were still whirling as she tried to find a solution; and the next, in spite of her intentions, Elinor was awake to the grey of a new morning and feeling no better. She was deep in misery as all her fears were only intensified. What would Ashton do?

To gain his inheritance, he had gone through a marriage ceremony — but that did not mean he must keep her. Perhaps he had never intended it. Presumably once the conditions of the will had been met, his inheritance would hold. There had been no mention yesterday of his wanting the right to protect her. Perhaps he no longer cared about that.

Mrs Haddon shook her head at the sight of Elinor's white and drawn face. Elinor tried to make her voice light. 'Do

I indeed look so worn and faded?'

'No wonder with the way you've been treated. But my dear, I have something important to tell you. And which may help you.'

Elinor felt a surge of hope. Had Ashton asked for her?

Mrs Haddon lowered her voice. 'Mr Charles has discovered who took you to London.'

Elinor stared at her. 'Who? Is it someone known to me?'

'I don't know. Mr Charles wishes to tell you secretly and at once. Sir Ashton will never know of it; you will be back without ever being missed, as he still sleeps late after his accident. And Haddon has one of the gigs all ready and waiting for you so you need not walk. The rain has stopped now; it rained heavily overnight while you slept but the mud need not trouble you. You need only agree.'

'Then of course I will go.' The kindly couple were making everything so easy for her; and if she could at last know the identity of her secret enemy, Ashton must surely listen to her.

Arriving at the small familiar house, she scrambled down without waiting for Haddon's assistance. Charles was at the door already. 'So you have come.'

'Yes.' She hurried in as Haddon closed the door behind her. 'I hear you have news for me.'

He nodded, partly to Haddon it seemed, who was still standing behind her. Elinor smiled at him. 'I cannot stay long.' Strange that Charles had not ushered her into the parlour. 'But I am sure I could sit down for a little while at least.'

'In a moment,' Charles said smoothly. 'Although when you hear who was behind your abduction, you may not be so eager to hurry back.'

Not Ashton? Fear tightened her throat. But why would he do such a thing? She mouthed his name.

'You have gone quite pale,' Charles said. 'No, not your husband. Although if you return to Ridgeworth, I cannot tell how this person is to be avoided.'

She sighed. 'I can decide that for myself.'

'And I do not know how you will convince Ashton of the truth. When you were in London, you were taken to the house of a Mrs Diamond, I believe?' And as she nodded, 'This lady has a stepson. Not that there is any love lost between them. But they know how to work together for mutual advantage when required.'

'I do not know anyone named Diamond. One of the servants at Ridgeworth? Someone we met in Salisbury? The false Reverend Greenwood?'

'She keeps her previous name for business purposes. No, the surname of her husband is Dixon. So her stepson is at present in your employ.'

Elinor felt the colour drain from her face. Oh, no. She had trusted him, even confided in him. And yes, he would protect Ashton with his life. But that did not mean the same loyalty would be extended to his new wife.

Many things were suddenly becoming clear. When Ashton had turned against her so abruptly, had Merrill informed Ashton that Dixon had returned from London? What had Dixon told him? She did not doubt now but that Dixon had lied, poisoning Ashton's mind against her. And the emeralds; doubtless Dixon had made sure that Ashton could see her take them. If Ashton had not woken, Dixon would have told him. And she had thought Dixon a reliable ally. *Fool*, she berated herself. She had fallen straight into Dixon's trap.

She thought, *I must tell Ashton. But he will never believe me. If I go back, I will be in danger.*

Charles said kindly, 'Your thoughts are clear in your face. A terrible dilemma for you. Still, before you think how you are to deal with this new knowledge, there is something I wish to show you.' He turned, gesturing towards the stairs.

Elinor said, 'Can you not just tell me? And I think I would like to sit down, please.' She must decide what to do.

'No time for that. Come.' Already he was taking her arm firmly and leading her upwards.

They were passing the room where she had recovered and, taking a rough flight, she had hardly noticed. 'I did not know these other rooms were in use.'

'Only when required. My apologies for the poor state of repair. Don't worry; I am sure it will not take long. I am an admirer of your ability to persuade.'

'I do not know what you mean. Persuade who?'

They stopped before a strong wooden door, recently repaired with stout planks. There was a large key prominent in the lock. Charles turned the key. 'Please enter.'

Elinor suppressed a gasp. 'You are not going to keep me a prisoner, surely?'

'I would not express it like that.'

Charles took her wrist again, pulling her onwards.

She could not escape; Haddon was so close behind her that she could feel his breath on her neck. She shivered. 'If you are hoping to ransom me, I doubt whether my husband will deem me to be of any value.'

'Nothing so crude. You are right. How would that gain us anything?' Charles laughed. 'This lock is not for you, as you will see. And your freedom will be regained with ease. There is only one small matter you have to achieve for me. Please, enter.' He spoke with exaggerated politeness and as if she had a choice.

There was no alternative. And perhaps whatever he wanted might be easily provided — but her rapid heartbeat did not confirm that hope. She looked down the long attic room which stretched the length of the house. It must have been where servants had slept, by the sight of several old straw mattresses on the floor. Once, it had no doubt been clean and dry enough; but now the whitewashed walls were grimed with cobwebs and peeling with damp. At the end of the room stood a single plain chair, incongruously clean. Green fire arranged across the wooden back: the emeralds.

She frowned, unable to understand. On the furthest mattress, there was a movement in what she had taken for a heap of old blankets. Her heart leapt in shock as she put her hands to her mouth. A guttural noise came from the bedding, making the flesh on her neck creep. 'What creature is this? Is it an animal? Is it in pain?'

Charles was expressionless. 'Go and look.'

Elinor put aside her fear in the need to help the poor thing. She took one cautious step and then another, quickening as the shape groaned again. A cry of anger, frustration and suffering. It was not an animal. She could see a pair of eyes glittering with anger, and a gaunt grey face partly obscured by a band of material tied over the mouth and chin to form a gag.

Elinor said, horrified, 'Charles, what has happened? Who is this?'

Charles had not moved to follow. He was still standing by the door, but his voice carried to her. 'This gentleman is the all-powerful arbiter of your fate, Elinor. Yours and mine also. Let me introduce you.' Charles walked slowly forwards, the heels of his boots echoing upon the bare wood. 'This is Sir Bartholomew Buckler, your husband's grandfather.'

14

'What? It cannot be.' Elinor swayed. She pushed her fingernails into her palms and the pain steadied her. She must not faint. She must stay clearheaded. She spoke calmly, although she felt like shrieking. 'This cannot be true. Sir Bartholomew is dead.'

Charles nodded. 'Everyone presumed so. As they were meant to.'

'But Sir Ashton has inherited the estate. And the title.'

'Indeed so. It would be most inconvenient for him were his grandfather to be still alive. No doubt he is aware of that.'

'No! You cannot mean that Ashton is responsible for this?'

Charles shrugged. 'What does it matter? We need to discuss what is to happen now.'

'You cannot keep him here like this.

You must release him.'

'I am afraid that is not possible. You see he has proved, shall we say, a little difficult. He does not seem to know where his advantage lies or to be amenable to persuasion.'

'He cannot even speak, bound like this. It is despicable. I would not keep an animal muzzled in this way.'

Charles smiled. 'A shame that Ashton does not appreciate you. What fire. What determination.'

Elinor sighed. 'What do you want?'

'It is very simple. Sir Bartholomew has only to sign a will leaving Ridgeworth to me.'

'How can that happen?' Elinor shook her head in disbelief.

'It is only fair. It should be mine. My family have held it for generations.'

'But you lost it in a game of cards. It is no longer yours.'

'Legally, no. But no man of honour would have held me to such a moment of foolishness. It is mine by right. And my terms are reasonable, as I have explained to him. While Sir Bartholomew survives, Ridgeworth can remain in his possession. I only ask that he leaves it to me. There can be no possible hardship in that. Not for him.'

'What about Ashton?'

'What about him? His grandfather cares nothing for him. He willed it to Ashton merely to spite me. Ah, I see. You are concerned about your position. Since your marriage to Ashton seems to be on very shaky ground now, it will surely be in your best interest to abandon Ashton and throw in your lot with me. I shall have no objection to such an arrangement.'

Elinor tried to keep her face still, hiding her feelings. How could Charles possibly think that? She longed to shout and scream *her* objections. Here, however, he was all-powerful. The only way to escape — and help his victim also — would be to convince Charles she was on his side and would do as he asked. She said, 'First you must allow him to speak. Or how can he agree?'

'He could have gestured his willingness to co-operate any time during the past few weeks. And he has had the opportunity when eating and drinking. But I suppose we must try this your way.'

'Good. Thank you. Otherwise there would be no sense in bringing me here.'

Charles nodded. 'I warn you, he is barely civil. You may not like what you hear. Haddon, stand close.' He approached the mattress, regarding its occupant for the first time since Elinor's arrival. 'I have given in to the lady's request. You are to have the chance to speak. Watch your vicious tongue, if you please.'

Elinor steeled herself for the flood of oaths that would surely come. She watched, hardly able to breathe, as Haddon produced a pocket knife and cut through the bonds at the old man's hands and feet. Lastly he cut the gag away. He stepped back smartly.

They were both fearful of him, Elinor

thought. But what could such an old, frail gentleman do to them? And further weakened by this cruel treatment as he must be. She walked up to the bed.

'Take care,' Charles said. 'Do not get too close.'

'If I am to talk to him, surely I must hear his replies? Besides,' she added, glancing at him with her heart contracting, 'what can he do? He is in a pitiful state.' She moved nearer.

Suddenly a claw-like hand shot out with the speed of a snake, gripping her wrist. 'I do not want your pity,' the old man hissed. 'I will show you what I can do.' His grip was surprisingly strong. He was swiftly pulling her closer; she could smell the sour scent of his breath. Before Charles could speak, Haddon was there, giving the old man a sharp blow on the arm; then he fell back, loosing his hold.

'I warned you,' Charles said. 'Perhaps now you will heed me. He neither wants nor needs your pity. Or deserves it. Removing him from the world would do everyone a favour. Now, can we progress?'

Elinor was shaking. She swallowed, her mouth dry. She whispered, 'I do not see why you think he will listen to me.'

Charles did not trouble to lower his voice. 'It was his idea for Ashton to undertake this marriage to you. A change of heart after a life of wickedness, supposedly. If that can be believed. But whatever his motive in including you, it may be of use to us.'

Elinor could not imagine those cold eyes holding anything as benign as a change of heart. But she had no option but to try. She stepped forwards again, this time being careful to remain out of reach. She was conscious also of Charles and Haddon behind her. She said with dignity, 'I would value some privacy if you please.'

'I am sure you would. But, you see, I am not quite certain that I can trust you either. I would rather hear all that is said.' Charles paused. 'We will stand back, at least. And do not forget, old man, that I have my duelling pistols to hand and will not hesitate to use one of them if required.'

The old man laughed. 'You are bluffing, Charles, as always. All you ever do.'

Elinor could hardly believe what she was hearing. 'Pistols? What are you saying?'

'Ah — when he first arrived, I offered him an honourable option. That of facing me in a duel. Once he has signed, of course. So far, he has not accepted.'

'Because it was only another bluff,' Sir Bartholomew grated.

'As you have not yet accepted my offer, we do not know, do we? Maybe I am offering this chance to see how strong is your desire for life. And how likely I am to gain your signature. Personally, I believe you do wish to survive and will take the chance. If you are the victor and manage to kill me, you may tear up the new document. Now, my dear Elinor, we shall withdraw a little. Pray begin.'

'Yes, do. I am anxious to hear your arguments.' The old man broke off, overcome by a fit of coughing.

'Charles, he needs water at least.'

'I need nothing from him.' The old man glared at her. 'And your concern does not impress me, if you thought it would. Come, your arguments, if you please. Entertain me.'

'I wish I could,' Elinor said briskly. 'How can I say anything sensible, let alone persuasive, when I have hardly recovered from the shock of your being here at all?' She took a breath, since no one seemed willing to answer this question. 'Well, I do not see why leaving Ridgeworth to Ashton should matter to you. The estate has belonged to Charles' branch of the family for generations and as far as I can gather, there have never been kindly feelings between your grandson and yourself.'

'Of course it matters. I won the game. Charles knew the risk he took in playing at all. And Ashton is of my blood. Whether I like him or not has nothing to do with it.' With difficulty, he raised himself on one elbow. 'You have told me nothing new. As I suspected, you know nothing of the real situation. How could you?' He was leering at her, an expression of wild triumph in his eyes.

'I do not understand you.'

'And Charles knows nothing of it either.'

Elinor stared at him. Behind her, she could hear Charles moving forward. He called out, 'Knows nothing of what?' His voice was strained.

'You thought you were so clever with your plan,' the old man gloated. 'You have taken such pleasure in telling me of it as it progressed. So clever to enlist your previous coachman and his cronies and replace Ashton's intended bride with her maid. Who once married, would do as she was told. Or would she? Maybe her loyalty would have been to Trigg and her own family rather than you. So even more cunning to betray your criminal partner and save the intended bride, so she would be forever in your debt. You'd encourage her to marry Ashton as planned, exert your charm and win her love, and dispose of Ashton. Convoluted, but possible. And if she proved intractable, you could always go back to your first plan. No one would miss her.'

Elinor gave a strangled cry, a hand to her mouth. No wonder everyone had told her how wicked this old man had been. How could he invent such a vicious lie? Yet so cleverly interwoven with the truth. She looked at Charles, waiting for his denial.

To her horror, he grinned. 'I am pleased that you have been attending fully. Not always easy to tell, with you.'

'A difficulty arose when you discovered your murderous attack had robbed her of her memory. But maybe not. It rendered her even more dependent on you.'

'Charles!' Elinor cried. 'You are surely going to deny these accusations?'

Both men ignored her. Charles laughed. 'She has no more lost her memory than you or I. She is a skilled actress. I was almost convinced at first. But she will be a fitting wife for me. What a partnership!'

Elinor felt herself to be in a waking nightmare. 'I *have* lost my memory.' Her voice was filled with pain. Surely Charles must believe her? She had a sudden flash of understanding. Charles had never believed her, because he always dealt in lies to achieve his own ends and had thought her the same. The kind and gentle rescuer she had trusted had never existed. He was as bad, if not worse, than the man on the mattress.

She pressed both of her hands to her face. Every instinct was urging her to shriek and scream her anger at this betrayal. But she was in his power and would endanger her safety even more if she opposed him openly. His actions were no longer rational, if they ever had been. Maybe losing his inheritance had tipped him into this state of mind.

She had no need to defend herself, it seemed. 'You are a fool, Charles,' the old man said. 'Of course she is telling the truth. I wondered when I first heard your tale; but now I have met her, I am quite certain of that. You, Charles, cannot recognise truth when you see it. And I am very glad to have met her. She is a delectable sight.' There was a lascivious look in his eyes that made Elinor shudder. 'However, Charles, I cannot follow your reasoning that her presence would persuade me to make a will in your favour.'

Charles sounded bored. 'Because you seemed to have had a weak moment in making the conditions in your will. It seemed you might be having an unusual attack of remorse. According to your lawyer.'

The old man turned to Elinor. 'My lawyer is in the pay of Charles also. You will hardly be surprised to hear that.'

She was beyond surprise. By now, she hardly knew what she was feeling.

'Remorse, however?' the old man continued. 'No, that was not at the root of my finding and naming this most beautiful young lady. I said you were a fool, Charles. More of a fool than you know. That card game, where I won Ridgeworth, was no random opportunity. I grew up knowing Ridgeworth rightfully belonged to my branch of our two families. In the mists of the years, Ridgeworth had changed hands and ownership several times. One side or the other. I decided to unravel the truth and discovered some surprising facts. Ridgeworth is more mine than yours and always has been.'

'Words. Meaningless,' Charles sneered.

The old man took no notice. 'Even so, both our claims stand for nothing against that of the true and rightful claimant.'

'I am not interested.'

'You should be. You had the solution in your grasp. Indeed I have it from Haddon that she would have married you, her saviour, the only person she knew and trusted at that time. And no, you denied her. You pushed her from you, to marry Ashton.'

'What?' Charles's voice was hoarse.

Elinor felt all the blood draining from her face, leaving her skin cold.

'This girl, Elinor, is the heir to Ridgeworth. It is all hers. And therefore could have been yours. But you made her marry Ashton. Therefore, it is now his.'

★ ★ ★

Ashton thought, *I am a fool. I will solve nothing lying here, feeling wronged. I need to talk to Elinor and without letting my anger get the better of me. And maybe she will forgive my unreasonable attitude so we may begin again.*

Dixon, however, came back alone and with a strange smile flickering briefly across his lips. 'She was seen leaving in the gig with Haddon and is not yet back.'

Ashton thought, *a fool twice over*. He sighed. 'She will return soon, as she has in the past.'

'That was several hours ago.'

Ashton sat up, all his senses alert once more. 'She has never been so long before.'

'Perhaps this time, she has gone for good.'

Dixon, he thought, did not seem to care too much. Ashton cared, and very much so. The prospect of losing her was painful to him. Only now did he realise just how much. He said steadily, 'I will not coerce her. She must decide what she wants to do.'

'I'm surprised you can ever trust her after all the evidence you have of where her loyalties lie. Stealing the emeralds. Back and forth to Charles. Hardly the actions of a true wife.'

'Even so, her actions have saved my life, as you know. Without her I would have been murdered after the fall. And you know yourself how such an obligation feels.'

Dixon shrugged. 'Not the same. You don't need to feel obligated to her forever.'

He said very quietly, 'This is not a matter of obligation, Dixon, but of choice.' He thought, *I must get up. Something is wrong. I can sense it.* He swung his legs from the bed.

Dixon was not looking at him, occupied in taking linen from a drawer. 'It is not what we planned. What we always spoke of.'

'What? I shall get dressed. Now.'

'I don't know what you think you can do. And you know what I mean about our plans. Leaving all the mess here behind. Going to the Americas as equals, starting a new life.'

Ashton stared at him, perplexed. 'But that was before Ridgeworth was restored to us. The one worthwhile thing my grandfather, evil man that he was, ever achieved. And even that by dubious means, but I have to be glad of it. I thought you were also glad. Regaining such an inheritance is everything.'

'Glad? Condemned to an existence of service against a life of freedom?'

'You do not have to be. Not at all.' Dixon was free to do as he chose but Ashton would not willingly see him return to the poverty of London's streets. 'I can make you my agent in Granger's absence, or you could try your hand at farming maybe. Whatever you like. I would never abandon you.'

Dixon was passing his clothes to him, his face dark. 'You don't understand me, do you? I would still be beholden to you.' He added, 'And after all I have done. Working in your best interests in ways you've never even guessed at. Fully occupied as you are in your new life as a landowner.'

Ashton regarded him with disquiet. 'I had no idea you felt like this.'

Dixon looked up, smiling suddenly. 'Don't pay any heed to me. You know me. Always grumbling.'

Ashton nodded. Later, he would deal with this. For now, something else had occurred to him. 'Where is Mrs

Haddon? Did she not go too?'

'No. She's still here. Do you want to speak to her?'

Ashton said slowly, 'She knows something then. I can guarantee it. But I believe something is about to happen here. I would rather wait and watch it unfold. And when it does, we shall be ready for it. Are you with me?'

Dixon's eyes were fierce with anticipation. 'Of course.'

15

The old man laughed and coughed, his face reddening as his shoulders heaved. He said again, 'Ridgeworth is Ashton's now. Through her.'

'You are lying.'

Elinor was still almost immobile with shock. Hers? Ridgeworth had always been hers? What madness was this? She turned to look at Charles, who was pale with fury.

The old man said, 'I am not.'

'Tell me that you are lying.' Charles raised his arm and Elinor realised with a jolt of horror that he was holding one of his pistols.

The old man coughed again, shaking his head. There was no mistaking his look of triumph. 'And while we are dealing in revelations, I have another bridal gift for you, Elinor. Tell your husband there was no family curse of sleepwalking and violence. I invented that to punish him for trying to marry without seeking my permission. But there is no danger to you.' He turned to Charles. 'Your sister was weak and sickly. Could have gone at any time. She would never have survived child-birth — so what use was she to my family and my line? A good thing that she slipped quietly away.' The old man laughed.

Elinor said hotly, 'That is cruel.'

Behind her, Charles said, 'Move aside.' There was madness in his voice, as if driven beyond endurance. 'So, old man. You have asked for this.' The noise of the shot in the enclosed space was like an explosion. Elinor screamed. The old man's face became rigid. He clutched at his chest, gasping for breath, and fell back onto the bed, his limbs twitching.

Mindless of her own safety, Elinor ran to him, kneeling in the dust beside him. There was no blood visible and he was still breathing. 'Where are you hurt?'

His voice was faint. 'Listen. Not much time. My wife's emeralds. Charles has taunted me about making you take them. Return them, if you do nothing else useful.'

'He said they were his mother's.'

'He fooled you, girl.' His breath rasped; the final effort made, he fell back and was still.

Elinor stood up, edging away as if in horror, until she could feel the chair behind her. 'You have killed him.'

Charles shrugged, thrusting the pistol into Haddon's hands. 'No. I shot wide.'

'But he is dead!'

Charles was looking down at the body. 'No great loss to the world or to any of us. There's no blood, no mark of a shot. No doubt he has suffered an apoplexy.'

'Brought on by your cruel treatment of him,' Elinor said indignantly. Easy to snatch up the emeralds and conceal them, once again, in her pocket. She must hope Charles did not notice they were missing.

'I bear no guilt for his death, I can assure you.'

Elinor was thinking swiftly. 'I can be of no further use to you here. There is no need for me to stay.'

'There is every need. We must reconsider and decide what to do next. An inconvenience, as I did not plan this — but he has given us valuable information, so we can now progress. Indeed, we are in a position of strength. Better, as he so helpfully informed me, if I had married you in the first place; but we merely return to my original plan: to dispose of Ashton so you can marry me. It is what you always wanted.'

But not what she wished now. There seemed little point in telling him this, however, or trying to reason with him. She too must decide what to do. Best to pretend to agree with him and gain his trust. Otherwise, she would be in no position to help Ashton. The cold and calculating way he talked of disposing of Ashton filled her with horror, but she must discover exactly how he meant to achieve this and seek to prevent him. She said, 'I intended to be a true and loving wife to Ashton, since that was required, but I fear you are right. I cannot make him love me and he has made it plain that he no longer wants me.'

Charles regarded her thoughtfully. She tried to hold his gaze without flinching. He said at last, 'He would have wanted you if he had known what you brought with you. No matter; his mistake. I will keep you beside me tonight. You may well be useful.'

She forced her voice to remain steady. 'What are we going to do?'

'You will discover that shortly. All in good time.'

'I will be more useful if I know the plan.'

'A risk I must take, I'm afraid.' He grasped her arms tightly, leading her down the stairs and out of the house. 'You have the gig ready again, Haddon?' As Haddon was seeing to the horse,

Charles was speaking with a sinister calm. 'Somehow, I do not feel I can entirely trust you. Before we arrive, I am afraid I must bind your mouth. I am sorry to submit you to this indignity but I need to be certain you will not try to interrupt matters by speaking out of turn. Or screaming a warning.'

Elinor shrugged. 'If you must. Why should you believe me? And I am sure it will not be for long.'

'No. Once you are free once more, the situation will be very different.'

Elinor knew his meaning. *Once you are a widow. Once Ashton is dead.* She held out her wrists. 'Maybe you should bind my arms too? To be completely certain in every respect.'

He paused, obviously disconcerted by her willingness to comply.

She said, 'But maybe I should climb into the gig first? It will be difficult afterwards.' She smiled. 'You would probably have to throw me in. I would rather you did not, if you do not mind.' All the time she was speaking so lightly, she was thinking, thinking. Haddon also was distracted, turning from the horse's head to see if Charles should need assistance. Would there be time, as she got in, to whip up the horse and drive off? Could she reach the house first and give warning? She was up and seated. It had to be now.

Suddenly, the shadowed tree trunks around them were filled with movement. A voice said, 'A word if you please. I am owed.'

She was too late. Already one man was at the horse's head, pushing Haddon aside. Who were they? She was trying to look in all directions at once. Were these the men who had waylaid them on the Salisbury road?

Charles said, 'What are you doing here?'

'Well might you ask me. You thought me safely out of your way, I'll be bound, sending me off into your trap.'

'Trap? That was none of my doing.'

'Nothing happened as we'd agreed it. *That* was of your doing.'

There were only four of them, Elinor realised, although that was bad enough. They were not here with any good intent. But she might yet be able to use this sudden appearance to her advantage, if she could keep her wits about her.

The spokesman was saying, 'And if I'd not been sent warning through Tom here, I too would be in a prison hulk, like poor Mary could have been. My own cousin's child.'

Charles snorted. 'There's no need for your 'poor Mary's.' You cared little enough about her when you left her to her fate. No warning for her, it seems.'

'We came to her rescue when needed. She bears no grudge.'

'Kindly don't talk about me as if I weren't here.' A woman's voice. One of the figures, whom Elinor had taken for a boy, stepped forward.

Trigg laughed. 'If I say you bear no grudge, that's what you'll do, my love.'

It was all Elinor could do to sit quietly, making no sound. She had to disguise her horror as she realised who this was. She was looking at the coachman, Trigg, who had attempted to replace Elinor with Mary. Who had ruthlessly tried to kill Elinor once already and almost succeeded. And Mary was here too. Of course she was. And the glances between them were far more than cousinly.

She thought, *Be calm; I can be in no danger now. If anything happens to Ashton, Ridgeworth must come to me. Ah, as long as Trigg knows this.*

She took a deep breath and spoke in the clearest, coolest voice she could muster. 'Charles! Who is this, please?'

It stopped all of them. Heads turned towards her in surprise; but for Trigg's part, also with recognition and contempt. 'Oh, it's you. The one we should have done for at the first. I think you know very well who I am.'

'I am afraid not. I have suffered a most unfortunate accident and cannot remember anything. I do not know what you are talking about.'

'Which is to your advantage,' Charles said. Whatever he believed about her loss of memory, he was quick to make use of it now. 'Obviously what cannot be remembered cannot be testified.'

'Ah. I don't know why you have her now but I say we should finish the job off and be done with it.' Trigg held a cudgel in one hand, tapping it against the palm of the other. Although she was sitting above him, Elinor could not avoid flinching as he raised it.

'You fool,' Charles said, grasping his arm. 'Without her, we have nothing. With Ashton dead and his wife also, who will inherit? I for one have no idea. I doubt whether Ashton has. The estate could be locked in chancery for years with only lawyers to benefit.'

Trigg stared at him. 'Don't try to gull me. It could go back to you.'

'No, it could not. Not unless Ashton willed it to me, and why would he do that? Believe that and you are more stupid than I thought. This is exactly why all the planning must be left to me.'

In spite of her situation, Elinor knew a flicker of grim amusement. She very much doubted whether Charles would reveal his greatest mistake in sending her to Ashton. And he did not.

Trigg frowned. 'So why is she here now?'

Elinor said quickly, 'Because I can see where my best advantage lies. I am not happy in my new marriage. When I am no longer married to Ashton, I will throw in my lot with Charles and Ridgeworth will become his.' She could see Trigg was still frowning. He was not yet convinced. She said crisply, 'And I can guarantee you will receive what was promised to you. I shall pay you myself.'

'We are wasting time,' Charles said. 'We are on our way to Ridgeworth now.'

'So we will come with you,' Trigg said. He grinned. 'Ensure nothing goes wrong. And one of my men can stay back with my fair lady here. Just to make certain of her.'

'No,' Charles said. 'We have experienced your methods of 'making certain' before. She stays with me. However, our movements at the house can only benefit from extra numbers. Except that you and your men must do as I say.' And as Trigg hesitated, 'Or there can be no result and no reward.'

Elinor held her breath. She could see the uncertainties flickering on Trigg's face as he tried to work it out. She could guess what he was thinking. This was not what he had intended. Not at all. But was there any alternative?

He said grumpily, 'Why take the gig? You will rouse the house with the wheels rattling and this horse neighing to his old stable mates as like as not. Or has my lady lost the use of her legs since being raised so high?'

'Stop your insolence,' Charles snapped. 'You are insulting my future wife. You had better remember that. And we shall leave the gig once we are within sight of the house.'

There was hope, Elinor thought, in this lack of agreement between them which must have saved her life in the beginning. And also Charles seemed to have forgotten to bind her mouth. Even now, as Haddon climbed up onto the groom's seat behind, Trigg was giving Charles a black look. 'You'll take Mary with you to watch her.'

'Not unless she sits with Haddon,' Charles responded sharply as he swung himself up to sit beside Elinor. Mary had hardly time to scramble up nimbly before Charles whipped up the horse and they set off at a canter, leaving Trigg and his men to break into an ungainly run behind them.

'Step lively now,' Charles called back to them. 'We'll take the quicker way.' Without pausing, he swung the gig off down a green track.

Haddon said, 'That bridge isn't safe for a horse.'

Charles laughed. 'The bridge has stood for years. It will outlive me. I'll not be swayed by old women's fears.'

He turned to Elinor. 'Take note as we cross. You will see where we seized the old man. You can note how the bank crumbles there. Easy to slip and fall. As two of my men were willing to testify.'

'But a body was found.' She had almost forgotten about that; Ashton had told her how he received the news just before she arrived.

'Not his, obviously. That was Granger, dressed in the old man's coat and boots with his signet on one finger. His death proved most useful.'

A chill ran down Elinor's neck. 'So you killed Granger?'

'I did not kill him, no. Trigg did that. You should know. You were there — but of course, your memory has gone. A convenient forgetting of anything unpleasant.'

It all made a horrible sense now. When Charles had said he would not be a party to this murder, he had obviously not been averse to murder in general, when it suited him.

Haddon shouted, 'Here's the bridge.'

Charles gave a hunting call as he brandished his whip. Beneath them, the planks creaked alarmingly. Elinor clutched at the side of the gig while Mary stifled a scream. And they were over. 'As I told you,' Charles sneered.

By now, Trigg and the others were barely in sight. Was this a good idea? Elinor thought. Would their anger at this treatment make them more violent? Or more likely to make mistakes, which maybe she could make use of?

Charles got down, still laughing and jeering back at them, as Haddon went to see to the horse. No one was taking any notice of her. She and Mary had the gig to themselves. It had to be now.

★ ★ ★

The trap was set. Ashton was determined Charles must be caught where there could be no escape. They would face him within the main bedroom where he would expect to find his victim sleeping and unaware.

Merill and other loyal servants were placed in the library, only to come out when the whole gang was cut off. Merrill had nodded stoutly enough, although Ashton had doubts of his usefulness when it came to it; he was employed as a butler not an armed guard. But Charles was his main target. Get him and the others would crumble. Dixon had said, 'You don't think he will come alone?'

'It's possible. But he's too much of a coward. I think he'll be back with Trigg again. That is my hope.'

Now Ashton and Dixon were in position in Ashton's bedroom, Dixon concealed behind the curtains looking over the drive and Ashton at the window towards the ridge where they might approach on foot. Would Charles come? After all the planning, this was the first time he had a few quiet moments to think. Maybe he had over-reacted. Maybe Charles was even now taking Elinor into his arms — or galloping off to a new life with her. No, why would he? He could have done that from the first.

Better to think about something else; they could have a long wait. Unbidden, Dixon's earlier remarks came into Ashton's mind. And one in particular. Ashton said, 'When we were talking earlier, what did you mean by saying you had helped me in ways I have not guessed at?'

To his surprise, Dixon did not reply at once. He had never known him at a loss for a ready response, however difficult the question. Ashton said, 'Dixon? Answer me. When you said you had dealt with those servants who were against us?'

'Yes. As I told you, some could be relied on to be with us. Some might not take any action, either for us or against, but they are harmless enough. Those who were a danger to us have gone, slowly but surely.'

'Granger was in the process of separating them out for me. Before he left.'

'Disappeared, more like. And through no wish of his. Find the site of the attack on the coach and you will doubtless find Granger's body not far away.'

'I have to agree.' It was the first time he had admitted that to himself. He must control his anger. That would only lead to errors of judgement and this time, for Charles, there must be no mistakes. And Dixon must not be allowed to distract him from his original question. 'I am of course grateful to you. And for everything you have done for me. But how did you persuade those others to go?' Ashton made his tone light, as of making conversation during the tedium of their vigil, keeping his watchful eyes focussed on the woodland. Across the corner of the room, he knew Dixon was doing the same. But some deep instinct was telling Ashton that the question was important.

Dixon answered him freely. 'I paid them a visit in the night. I made sure they understood what might happen to them if they stayed. Cowards, all of them. It was easy enough.'

Ashton thought not all were cowards. A deadly realisation dragged at his heart as everything became clear. Elinor had been telling the truth about her night-time attacker. He said, with ice in his voice, 'Did you resent my future wife so much?'

Dixon turned. The two men stared at each other across the room. Dixon attempted a laugh. He knew what was meant, Ashton thought, and was making no attempt at a denial. 'It was more of a test. Which she passed.'

No. Add to that, Dixon's reaction less than an hour ago when talking of their future plans. Or what Dixon had seen as plans. To Ashton it had been a possibility, plucked from the prospect of an empty future, not wishing to be beholden to his grandfather for any-thing. A young man's idle dream, easily abandoned when there was no further need of it. But Dixon had not seen it that way.

Ashton closed his eyes in pain. He thought, but could not bring himself to voice it: and what of Sophia, his first wife? Dixon as silent as a cat. Not intending harm as such, merely to threaten and discourage. For a frail girl with a weakness of the heart, his actions must have had fatal consequences.

He recalled that time, after his first marriage. The young couple had been exploring their new happiness together. Sophia had been very much in love with him; he was pleased by how she was adjusting to a very different life. Dixon, he remembered, had warned him against it, convinced that the new bride would be all tears and complaints. Also there had been the flickers of resentment in Dixon's face as he muttered that obviously he was no longer needed. But he had stayed.

Ashton had hardly noticed. He had been so caught up in self-righteous zeal, convinced that this marriage would bring both sides together and end the feud. All of these clues were now congregating in Ashton's mind as damning evidence. He said, almost whispering, 'You always resented both of my wives. Sophia's death. It was you.' Hoping even now that Dixon would deny it.

Dixon said, 'I would give my life for you. You know that.' His head twitched suddenly to one side, back to his view of the drive. 'They are coming.'

16

Elinor stood up, snatched at the whip and cracked it in the air above the broad back and haunches before her, taking hold of the reins just in time as the gig jerked forwards. The horse seemed to have taken fright. Clinging on to the seat as well as she could, she swayed dangerously near the side but managed to stay on. As did her companion.

'What are you doing?' Mary shrieked. 'You'll kill us both.'

Elinor was still trying to cope with the shock of it herself as she tried to guide the gig in the right direction. To her surprise, her thoughts were cool and calm. Fortunately, the horse seemed to be making for the house; doubtless in the past he had been this way many times. Somehow she must dispose of Mary, who was now trying to climb over from the rear seat to grab at the reins. She tried to knock the other girl off balance, causing the horse to swerve in panic.

Now he was careering round the side of the house, grazing a wheel at the corner. As the gig lurched, Mary clutched at Elinor's arm as Elinor, with all the force she could gather, tried to push her off.

Screaming, Mary fell; surely they must now overturn? Yet somehow she stayed upright and as suddenly as he had begun, the horse stopped at last. Elinor felt bruised all over. She was shaking as she looked round. By the corner, Mary was lying on the cobbles but moaning softly. Already she was lifting her head. No time to worry about her now. Her lover and his friends were all too close behind. Leave her to them.

Surely someone in house or stables must have heard the noise? But all was quiet.

'Good boy,' Elinor said, her voice

quavering. 'Keep still, while I get down.' But the horse was standing meekly, head bowed. A different creature to the one who had swept her along on that wild ride. No time to be thankful for her safe arrival. She had to get inside before Charles and the others caught up with her. There would be no one about at this hour to let her in.

The door ahead of her must lead to the kitchen passage, or so she hoped. Where was the side door she had used? No time to look for it now; and besides, following her instructions, that would be locked and bolted too. If so, she must break a window. No one would hear in time if she relied on knocking. She put a hurried hand to the kitchen door — and almost overbalanced as it opened; she had hardly touched it. 'Mrs Haddon! Oh, thank goodness.' She stared at her in relief and surprise. Mrs Haddon, her good and trusted friend. Everything would be well.

'Come in, quickly.' Mrs Haddon gave

her a brief smile. 'Where is Mr Charles?'

'I lost him — but he will be here any moment. I must warn Sir Ashton.'

'Ssh,' Mrs Haddon hissed. 'You will wake the house and ruin everything.'

Elinor stared at her. She knew, suddenly, the full extent of her own foolishness. Mrs Haddon, whom she had trusted so much and wholly relied upon. Naturally Mrs Haddon would be loyal to her husband. And Charles.

Mrs Haddon was staring back at her. It seemed that she too was revising her thoughts. 'Lost Mr Charles? By design, it seems.'

Behind them came the pounding of footsteps, rounding the house and crossing the yard. 'Hold her!' Charles called.

Before the older woman could react, Elinor almost leaped past her, pushing her to one side. She ran down the stone-flagged corridor, tugged at the heavy door at the end — and thankfully, was into the entrance hall.

At last, a room she knew.

Horror welled in Elinor's throat as she ran up the stairs. If Charles got there first, he would kill Ashton. She was certain of that. And he must not. She loved her husband. Whatever the danger, she could not let this happen. She could hear the pounding of footsteps behind her.

She ran down the landing and burst into Ashton's room. As she tried to adjust to the contrast of darkness and moonlight, she saw that the window curtains were open. The room seemed to be filled confusingly with dark shadows and slivers of brightness. She screamed, 'Ashton, wake up!'

What happened next hardly seemed to make sense. Behind her, her pursuers were within the room, pushing her aside as they made for the bed. At the same time, two figures came from behind the opened curtains at the window, one with a sword in his hand. The metal caught the silver light as he held the blade to his assailant's throat.

The second was grappling with another of the intruders.

Even as she saw all this and realised, gladly, that Ashton had not been taken unawares, strong arms caught at her from behind, a hand at her neck crushing her painfully. 'Quiet, you fool. Would you ruin everything?' She knew without seeing his face. It was the voice that had wanted to avoid her murder, the voice that had become so familiar to her. Charles, who was now bent on betraying her. She tried to bite his hand but his grip was too strong.

He said, 'Drop your blade, Ashton, or I will kill her.'

Ashton's eyes were fixed on the other man's face. 'And what will you gain by that?'

'I lose nothing. She has proved less useful than I thought. A weak link in the chain.'

'I do not believe you.'

'Do you not?' Charles pulled Elinor backwards, out through the doorway, muttering in her ear as he did so. 'Hush, sweetheart, it will all be for the best. Pretend to be terrified.'

There was hardly any need for pretence. She rolled her eyes, managing only a strangled grunt. Charles was still moving. She stumbled, trying to shake her head at Ashton, unable to take her eyes from the blade only a few inches away from her face as Charles held her before him.

But Ashton too shook his head in defeat, obviously unable to take the risk. He lowered his sword. Charles released his hold and she twisted away from him — as Ashton feinted skilfully and pierced his opponent's shoulder. Charles shouted something in anger as he lunged after her, catching her arm to send her off balance. She stumbled and fell, knowing only the stone-cold hardness of impact as her head struck the topmost marble stair. And was into darkness.

★ ★ ★

Ashton went cold as a fury such as he had never known filled his heart. Every instinct drew him to Elinor, to hold her in his arms, to see whether she was still alive. But he knew with instant clarity that if he did so, he would endanger both their lives. He would be vulnerable and Charles would seize his chance. He said fiercely, 'You have killed her.'

'I did not intend to. You should have dropped your sword.'

Ashton advanced across the landing, his sword now aimed at Charles's heart. He said in a low voice, 'You will regret this.'

Charles looked round as if seeking escape. 'It's your fault. You as good as killed her yourself. She would have been safe with me. She should not have wriggled away. It wasn't what we intended. It was all part of our plan. I would have protected her.' Charles's voice was rising as he backed away.

'You and she never had any plan. I should have trusted her.'

'But you will not kill me? In cold

blood? I am defenceless.'

'You have broken into my house and attacked my wife. I have every right to kill you.'

'See, I mean you no harm now. Let me go quietly. I will cause no more trouble. You have my word.'

'Your word is worthless and always has been. But I will not kill you in cold blood, as you put it. We will fight.'

Charles hesitated. 'I agree.'

'Dixon, bring us another sword, if you please.' Ashton heard Dixon behind him and turned slightly, without taking his eyes fully from Charles. But his opponent had sensed the lack of concentration. Charles twisted away and leapt for the stairs, over Elinor's prone form. At that same moment, Elinor moved, trying to rise as she tugged at something in her pocket. As she shifted, Charles slipped on her skirts and the emeralds; he reached out to her, trying to steady himself. Elinor, still dazed, clasped her hands around his legs and they both fell together down the full length of the marble staircase.

★ ★ ★

Elinor lay still, winded by this further fall but amazed to be still able to breathe. She moved her legs a little and her arms. She was bruised and shaken but thankfully, she did not seem to be badly injured. She had come to rest on Charles, her head on his chest. He must have broken her fall. Cautiously she lifted her head to look at his face and saw that his eyes were wide and still.

From the landing above her there were urgent footsteps on the stairs, half-leaping and half-running. She thought, *Ashton?* And also with a slow gladness, *I remember. I know who I am.*

Yet there was no time to appreciate this discovery. A loud voice close to her ear shouted, 'Get the door open, woman. Now.' Rough hands were pulling her to her feet, with no enquiries as to whether she might be injured or not. She was slung over someone's shoulders. She knew who it was; she recognised the voice and the smell of horses about him. This was Josiah Trigg, Ashton's coachman, who had already attacked her once and would not mean her well now.

He was carrying her as if she weighed nothing. As he ran through the door, she glimpsed Mrs Haddon holding it open, her face white and fearful. Bemused by the rough treatment, Elinor could hardly think — and yet she must. What was Trigg going to do with her? Where was Ashton? She gripped at the dark greasy hair and pulled, hoping to slow him. 'Where are we going?'

He swore and then laughed. 'Not far. Or you're not.' He was panting a little, but speaking had no effect on his pace. 'Should have killed you at the first. This mess is all your fault.'

'You will not kill me — please.' She knew he would, but she must try to distract him. Behind them, as they bounced and lurched along with her head banging against his back, she could see the others in pursuit. She gasped, 'You will be hanged for it.'

'I'll be hanged anyway — but I'll have to be caught first. And they'll be delayed, trying to pull your body from the river.'

The river? Yes, they had reached the bridge. Already she could hear the planks beneath his boots. For the first time, as the pursuers gained on them, she could see them clearly. Dixon was approaching the bridge too. Ashton, making a heroic effort to keep up but still limping from his recent injuries, was only a short distance behind.

Trigg turned, laughing again, as he dropped Elinor onto the handrail; she felt a sharp blow to her back and was dizzy with pain. The planks were vibrating now with the tread of Dixon's boots. As Trigg bent to seize her feet and tip her over, the rail creaked and then broke.

There was a loud cracking and

splintering across the length and breadth of the bridge as the whole structure collapsed. Elinor was briefly aware of Trigg falling with her among the splintering timbers before she was immersed in the cold shock of the fast-flowing water.

★   ★   ★

Ashton, cursing his injured leg, saw the bridge go, taking Elinor, Trigg and Dixon with it. A great wave of fury propelled him forward. Amongst the tumble of rotten wood, he could see the three heads breaking the surface. But as he threw off his coat, he was concentrating on Elinor. She was in the middle of the fast-flowing current and he saw her hands clutching at a tangle of floating branches, caught fast on some unseen obstacle. How long would they hold?

And that might not be the only danger. Ashton spared a swift glance for Trigg — but already the coachman was being swept away, with a scream of terror. Dixon had fallen close to the bank but was not attempting to save himself. Instead, he was striking out towards Elinor.

To help her? Or harm her? Dread chilled Ashton's heart. He paused on the brink, took a deep breath and dived in. Aided by desperation, he covered more distance than he could have hoped. Also, once in the water, his injuries did not impede him. In moments, he was beside her. She opened her eyes wide, her face white, and smiled at him. He slid an arm beneath her shoulders, sharing her grasp on the branches to gather his strength, knowing they would not stay caught for long.

He turned, looking for Dixon. Now that Ashton had reached Elinor, there was no question that Dixon would help them both. There was no sign of him. Good, he must have got himself out after all. Ashton looked upwards, scanning the bank, expecting to see the resourceful Dixon holding a long branch or something similar for Ashton to catch hold of and pull them both out. Nothing.

Ashton turned his attention to the water, gauging the flow and direction of the current, knowing how dangerous this river could be — as his grandfather had found to his cost. Not too far away, at the bend of the river, he could see a tangle of jutting roots protruding from the bank. If he could dislodge their refuge of branches himself, maybe he could use them to push sideways to catch on to those roots. An immense risk, but it could work. And he dared not wait any longer for help to arrive.

He shouted to his wife, 'Trust me. Hold on.' She nodded. The branches rocked as he tugged at them. She followed his lead, gripping with both hands and pulling in the same rhythm. With a last heave, the branches jerked free and they were at the mercy of the water. Now Ashton must kick as strongly as he could, trying to guide the flotsam in the right direction.

The branches tossed and leapt as if alive, pulling against him, seeking the centre of the river. The roots were very near. If he missed them, they would be swept on; he did not know how long he would be able to hold Elinor above the water. He must not miss. Now, it had to be now. He twisted his whole body abruptly and felt Elinor moving with him, adding her strength to his. Yes, they were turning, a little. Would it be enough?

For one horrifying moment, he was sure they would fail. With a jarring thud that set his whole arm and shoulder shaking, the branches caught — and stopped. Waves surged over Elinor's face. Summoning one more burst of strength he did not know he had, Ashton pulled Elinor's head and shoulders out of the water. Her eyes were closed.

At last there was a figure above him reaching down to them. Dixon, he thought. He had come through in the end. Ashton summoned a grin, meaning to say, jokingly, 'Why the delay?' And found himself looking into the confused and loyal face of Merrill.

* * *

Elinor knew she was safe. She lay with her eyes closed. Once again, the comfort of a soft bed and clean sheets beneath her. But nothing else was the same as the last time. She said carefully, 'Ashton?'

Ashton said, 'I am here, my love. And you are safe.'

She smiled her relief and said slowly, 'I know who I am and what happened. I was thrown from the coach. They intended to kill me.' Her face clouded. 'And they had already killed Granger, poor man.'

'Yes, I am afraid so. But that is all in the past.' He paused, smiling. 'There have been a great many alarms and dangers since that happened.'

She smiled too. 'Yes, I know.'

'Are you sure? Do you also recall everything else that happened after your first accident? And that you are now my wife?'

'To fulfil your grandfather's wishes. Yes, I remember all of that.'

'It has all come back to you? This is wonderful news.'

She sighed. 'Is it? After all the lies I told you? Can you forgive me?'

'There is no need. I am the one requiring forgiveness. My behaviour was insufferable. I should have been more understanding about your predicament. I should have told you about my first wife from the beginning. Considering the possible dangers, I should never have agreed to comply with my grandfather's conditions.'

Elinor said softly, 'Charles told me about your wife. I am so sorry.'

'I know. I never loved her but I had a fondness for her.' His face was bleak. 'She did not deserve to die like that.'

Elinor said quickly, 'Your grandfather lied. It was not your fault. There was no inherited tendency for sleepwalking and violence. Another example of his vicious malice and mischief-making. He admitted as much to me when we were imprisoned together.'

'Yes. I know that now.' He paused, his face dark. 'And I also know who was responsible for Sophia's death. And who first told you of it. And threatened you in the night. It was Dixon.'

'Dixon?' Elinor's eyes widened. 'But Charles told me Dixon was responsible for abducting me. If Charles was telling the truth about that.'

'This time, I expect Charles was. Well, Dixon is no longer a threat. He drowned when the bridge collapsed.'

'You could not save him?'

'I chose to save you.'

She saw the pain in Ashton's face and did not enquire further. 'I am so sorry.' She paused before saying softly, 'But Ashton, I am not frail. My heart is sound. I am happy to live a full married life with you, if you wish to keep me.'

He took her hands in his. 'Of course I

wish to keep you. How can you doubt it?'

'And Ashton, there is something else Sir Bartholomew said, just before he died.' She put a hand to her eyes, recalling the horror of that moment. 'Oh, of course, you do not know. If you go to the cottage, you will find his body.'

'Hush. I do know. It is all done. Haddon has given me the full story now, of everything he knows.'

'Everything?' She took a deep breath. 'Did he tell you your grandfather claimed that Ridgeworth belonged to me?' She shook her head. 'And yet it may well be another lie. Even when I could not remember who I was, I began to suspect something was wrong when I found my mother's testament. You had accepted the affidavit, but my mother's name was different. She was Amelia Wellspring, not Elizabeth Aysgarth. And she never told me directly of any inherited wealth, although there were hints of descent from an old proud family. I thought she was fantasising.'

He took her shoulders, staring into her face. 'Do you know, I no longer care much about Ridgeworth. I am only concerned about you. You matter to me. You can have no idea how much I love you, Elinor.' He smiled. 'Even if I must call you Nell. And I behaved very badly towards you.'

'No, you had good reason. I should never have trusted Charles.'

'Why not? Charles could be infinitely charming when he chose and you were in a most vulnerable state, in no position to disbelieve him.' He gave a short laugh. 'And I am no better. Why did I accept the Haddons so easily?'

'I know. And Mrs Haddon was so kind to me.'

'Their loyalty was always to Charles, not you or me. She knew your recovery and success here would eventually benefit Charles. Apparently she had been his nursemaid years ago when the family were in London. But she left their employ to marry Haddon.'

Elinor said, 'I should not have been so willing to trust without thought.'

'Of course you should. It is one of the things I love about you. But I would hope you are able to trust me, although I hardly deserve it.' His face was close to hers. She closed her eyes as he kissed her. She had longed for this moment but the blissful reality surpassed all she might have imagined.

At last he said, 'So you are content to remain my wife?'

'Of course. There is no need to ask.'

'And will entrust me with your inheritance? Do not concern yourself over the truth of that. If my grandfather discovered it, I can too. And I will, have no doubt of it. But in this instance, I think I believe him.'

She shuddered. 'Ridgeworth? It brought us together, but after all that has happened here I would be happy never to see it again. How can I be grateful for an inheritance which has brought years of anger and hatred?'

He nodded, his face solemn. 'I agree.

And I was as much at fault as any. I was brought up to regard Ridgeworth as my right, at any cost.'

'You should not reproach yourself too much. You tried to end the feud, through your first marriage.'

'And made everything worse. After the death of his sister, Charles hated me more than ever. And when he lost Ridgeworth to my grandfather, I believe it was more than he could bear. But that is over with now; we must think only of ourselves and our own lives.'

Elinor smiled. 'You are right. We are free.'

★ ★ ★

Three years later, they stood overlooking the rolling aspects of downs and woodlands she had loved from the first. Ashton had kept his promise and they had returned to the village of her birth for the full ceremony and renewal of their vows. She had been surrounded with well-remembered faces from her childhood for what had been a joyous occasion. Their marriage was now complete.

Ashton said, 'You have endured a succession of rented properties without complaint. And here is your reward.' Before them a new Ridgeworth had risen from the old, completely rebuilt and hardly recognisable.

'We could not have stayed at Ridgeworth as it was, could we? Not with all the tragic memories. But this is more than I ever hoped for.' She gave a sigh of pure happiness. 'I could not wish for a better place or a more beautiful home.'

'Nor I. We are accepted now, and in no small part thanks to you. We will be happy here.'

She would be happy anywhere with him. From the first, when Ashton had told her what he had planned for Ridgeworth, Elinor had been only too pleased to agree. And with their new house completed, the future lay bright before them. Ashton said, 'Our home at last, and to be filled with our heirs — and none of this of my grandfather's choosing. He never intended such happiness for us.'

'No.' For a moment she almost felt sorry for the old man, alone and unloved, devoting his life to causing misery for everyone around him. But he had failed.

Ashton offered his arm. 'Shall we go in?'

Elinor nodded, smiling, and knowing the first of the heirs he spoke of would be arriving sooner than he knew. She would keep the knowledge to herself for just a few precious moments more. A joyous announcement to mark their new life and their love together, setting the seal on their future happiness.

THE END